Kaleidoscope

Kaleidoscope

Padma Jha

ISBN:	Softcover	978-1-4828-3529-8
	eBook	978-1-4828-3528-1

To order additional copies of this book, contact
Partridge India
000 800 10062 62
orders.india@partridgepublishing.com

www.partridgepublishing.com/india

CONTENTS

ONE

Diwali Shopping

Meena and Raghu stood in a corner of the brightly illuminated shop looking around. It was a sight that evoked admiration in their hearts. The shop had been decorated and modeled just for Diwali and to them it resembled the Tajmahal. The variety of sweets on display had been decorated to look like various seasonal flowers; and the rows upon rows of delicious goodies made them wonder what to buy. There were so many things to choose from!

The couple gazed on for some time and to the shop assistant it seemed that they were on the verge of a decision. On a closer look the couple seemed a prototype of the Indian middle class household, the fixed salary type with budget constraints. Luckily for Meena and Raghu the sweets and savories had their rates displayed on a fancy looking stand on each shelf, they would not have to ask the price of each one and feel embarrassed. They decided on half a kilo of laddoos, the cheapest sweet available in the shop.

Meena moved closer to the counter and told the attendant," "Half a kilo laddoos." The attendant looked at her disdainfully as he put away kaju rolls in a glazed container. He did not answer, just pointed toward the entrance. Meena was confused but another man came and he told her to make the payment first and get the required coupon. As she was paying Meena saw a smart Scorpio driving up, a couple just their age emerged from it, oh but what a difference! As against Meena's salwar kameez bought at the local sale, with the display "all suits 150 to 250", the woman from the Scorpio wore Calvin Klein jeans, designer top and funky jewellery. She did not even glance at the men at the counter who gaped and involuntarily made space for her.

The demeanor of the head attendant underwent a sea change as he obsequiously wished her in English. To her demand of "the best gift packs" a huge golden packet was shown, with neat rows of all the sweets displayed. Without enquiring about the price she ordered "Put twenty five of those in the Scorpio outside". She looked around the shop now in a bored manner while the man lit a cigarette and paced restlessly. The two attendants became busy in packing and putting away the gift packs.

"Half a kilo laddoos, please" – this time Meena spoke in a firm tone but the attendants did not even glance at her. She looked at her husband, frustrated. Raghu came up and taking her arm gently guided her out of the shop to their parked scootie. She sighed as he said, "Let's find a place which caters to people of our kind."

They stopped at the shop round the corner. It was not air conditioned but the shopkeeper welcomed them with a smile. Here too there were rows and rows of sweets sans the fancy price stand. Meena asked the price of a few and concluded that apart from laddoos she could also afford to buy gulabjamuns. The attendants were quick, their method brisk and polite, not fawning, the sort who believed that after hard work there is little room for obsequiousness.

Meena and Raghu came out of the shop with a smile on their lips, Raghu pleased with the content look on his wife's face. Yes, he was man enough to provide enough for his loved ones.

The Scorpio passed them and they looked at each other. That was their kind of Diwali shopping and this was their kind.

TWO

The Missed Opportunity

Rohit Agrawal lay sunk in the cushions of his luxurious car, mulling over the day's events. It had been a very successful day, no doubt soon he could be the principal share holder of that steel factory and then there was no looking back. His shoulders ached and his temples throbbed but these feelings of fatigue were just a reminder of his impending victory.

Another red light! At this rate he would reach home minimum one hour later than expected! He looked out of the window at the countless, nameless creatures hurrying, this was all that life was – hurry and hurry. He wondered what sort of life they led. Well- whatever sort they led, it did not matter- he himself had a perfect life, a "nice" wife who had brought a good dowry, and was passably good looking and did not ask too many questions; two healthy sons, what more could a man want? A beggar whined at his side and just then, a flash of a white dupatta sailed in front, the profile of a face was seen and within seconds the business tycoon had forgotten his empire, his wife and even his sons, had opened the door of his car and run after the familiar flash of white. The aghast driver did not know what to do, then he thought it better to remain in the car. But Rohit Agrawal had transformed- he had turned into that old Rohit, the innocent one whose head was full of ideals and a heart replete with dreams for he felt that had seen 'Her'! Dodging scooters and cars, shopping bags and shoppers, arousing the wrath of bus drivers and in general creating quite a stir, Rohit rushed after the white clad figure. Just as he thought he would not be able to catch up, he caught up with her, panting like a dog. He was certainly out of shape!

"Excuse me", he said and she looked back and all the castles that he had built in that short run tumbled and left him devastated. It was somebody else- not "She'. What had happened to him- the hardened businessman that he was- how could he behave like a teenager in the afternoon of his life? He turned back ashamed. He must have run a long way because the way back to the car seemed so long and his steps were leaden. When he sank back into the cushions, a long sigh escaped him-he felt something hot prickling behind his eyelids, were they tears? But Rohit Agrawal could not shed any- he was too practical to do such foolish things- what happened today then?

Yes, it was like a wound that had healed on the surface but the scar was there too, each time he received a jolt, the wound broke open again revealing its rawness and there was no way he could find to heal it once for all. He turned to events that had happened around a decade and a half ago. He had just completed his MBA and had thought of setting a chain of small scale industries that would help eradicate unemployment. His father called him a fool but his mother and sister just doted on him. He was quite idle those days, he wanted to relax, settle and then think over ideas. His father had very grudgingly given in. Just as his father would leave for the factory, Rohit would don his trendiest clothes, take out his red Maruti and go for long drives. Those were the days! The monsoon had just set in and the cool showers were just the thing for a chap. He would take a short cut past a women's college whenever he felt he would be late for lunch. The old man was such a stickler for punctuality that he'd raise hell if anyone was even a few minutes late in reaching the dining room; he himself treated it as a matter of life and death and so would always arrive on the dot.

Every time he passed the college, instinctively, he would crane his neck to see if any "presentable" faces were around. Most of the times he was sorely disappointed- they were all well groomed no doubt but there was not much else and their over dressing irritated him. Why did they all look the same? That day's watch for pretty faces proved a problem as he did not see the road ahead and was nearly going to run over somebody when he braked just in time, the car skidded to a halt barely grazing the ankles of a girl. He jumped out apologizing profusely and bent to gather the books that had fallen to the ground. *Hamlet, The Way of the World, Metaphysical poetry, Emma,* So the girl was an English Honours student. "I am really very sorry" he said handing her the books- she accepted them regally and without displaying any emotion nor showing any feeling she turned around and walked away. He stood rooted to the ground- what Madonna had he seen! He ran after her shouting, he felt like a village oaf- "Miss oh miss please wait, I will drop you home." She turned around, as cool as an icicle- "That won't be necessary," she said and walked away.

Lunch time was something he did not realize took place, he could not think, he could not focus on any object, he even felt that he had become quite deaf for all that he could see was one cool face, very fair; and all that he could hear was "That won't be necessary". His sister pinched him sharply and he awoke to reality- his father was concluding the monologue with-"he was completely lazy earlier but now he has become a dullard also." So these epithets were for him! Doesn't matter! As long as the world contained that face and that voice, did anything else matter?

Next morning he woke up feeling elated. Even the cawing of the crows seemed sweet and the incessant downpour romantic. Getting up in the morning had a cause now- there was a proper mission in life now and he decided on a cream colored shirt and blue jeans- cool and casual and the girl would not realize that he had taken trouble to look good.

He parked his car a little distance away from the college- no point in bumping into his sister who attended the same college. He waited and waited- no sign of the cool miss- would she not come? He was on his twelfth cigarette when an auto rickshaw stopped and she stepped out. He observed her closely- hair swept back and held with a barette, pale blue salwar –kurta, no trace of make up, no jingle jangle anywhere, why did she remind him of the Indianised version of the Madonna, or Mary? There was something peaceful about her face, a radiant glow to it; he felt as if it was the inner beauty of the mind which had slowly entered her face. She paid the rickshaw and he advanced with an "Excuse me". He was sure that she had heard him but she did not say anything and walked inside the college gates. No point going there after her- their Principal was known to chew trespassers of the opposite sex alive, so he drove around till he thought it was the time she usually left. The trouble created by his absence in the dining room was completely forgotten.

At last, around four, she came out, who was this with her? A tall very pretty girl with laughing eyes accompanied her- definitely the younger sister- they had the same forehead and eyes. He again moved forward- "Please miss,"- the younger sister turned but Madonna walked off. This was surely a snub, he had to get the message that she did not want him near- but how rude! Couldn't she just listen once? May be she had a boyfriend- and he had a sudden urge to slowly and surely strangle the guy.

He went home dejected, the front door was closed and he kicked it- it was not latched and much to his embarrassment he saw quite a crowd in the drawing room- his mother's friends. The old biddies would go on gossiping and he would have to "see" another well- fed, well dowried girl from his community, just to say another "no". Today was just not his day. His sister came into the room with a tray. As he munched the samosas she observed him quietly and then asked, "Who is she?"

"Who is she?" what was this moron talking about? God! Had she seen him running after 'Her'? Outwardly he merely blustered, the best defence is offence, you see. She was quite persistent and then he decided to tell her. She was quite understanding and sympathetic when she heard his Madonna's description. "Yes, she is a senior- very dignified, the serious sort." No, she had not heard that she had a boyfriend; yes she lived in the colony not very far off, yes she would find the house number.

The wretched girl had fever the next day so he decided to do some sleuthing on his own. Next day when she left for home, he followed her auto rickshaw, being careful to keep two vehicles between them, no point in giving her the impression that he was the Roving Romeo sort. He found where she lived. There was a very old couple who waited eagerly for the girls it seemed, but there was a young man too.

Now, who could he be? He had to find out. He waited in the evening and saw the milkman- it cost him twenty rupees but the relief was worth a million bucks- the young man was an uncle, a medical student who stayed away most of the time. Obstacle cleared. He went home satisfied with the day's work.

Every day he would wait near the college gates only to be ignored. It hurt terribly and did irreparable damage to his ego but what else could he do? He had to see her and this was the only way. Once he had a wild impulse to ask the old gentleman formally (he had found out that he was her grandfather) if he could speak to her. He was saved from further humiliation for his sister told him that where his granddaughter was concerned, the old gentleman was very fierce and considered young men as "polluting influence". Well, that option was ruled out then.

Once while he was slowly driving around, she came before her usual time. She was alone- this chance mustn't be lost. He leaped out and stood squarely in front, blocking her way. He could not speak and remained tongue tied for a few seconds and she watched him- was there a hint of a smile? "You see, I must know your name," Why did he say that? He knew it- it was Urvashi-"I mean I must know about you, you have to talk with me, I wait here hours for you and you just walk off." Why was he perspiring so much?

She looked stern. A stray hair caressed her cheek and his only desire was to put it back in place. What was she saying? She had a sweet voice but did she need to add steel to it? "Sir," Sir? He? How could she address him as if he were a friend of her father's? "I am a student and may be you are one too. I have to make a career for myself so I would advise you not to waste time in all this." all this? She called his all-consuming passion for her, "All this"? She hailed a passing rickshaw and was soon carried away while he stood in a daze. Dinner time was a disaster. After his customary two chapattis, his father told his mother, "Your son has taken to eve teasing these days. Justice Shukla went to fetch his niece from college and there was this Lothario pouring his heart out to a girl. How Shukla enjoyed relating this at the club! Its final now. This loitering cannot go on. Tell the Tibrewalas to find an auspicious day for engagement- they have a fine girl. Leaving a bull too long without a noose is inviting problems." He left after uttering Rohit's death sentence.

It was a death sentence. He could not live without seeing her, let her reject him-he'd pursue her till she gave in, there had to be a way. As far as the noose was concerned, he'd put a real one around his neck if he was forced in such matters, he told his mother. His sister promised "to do something."

Meanwhile, poor Rohit thought such things happened only in movies to the Amir Khan types, but he was, Rohit Agrawal, B.Sc., MBA- most eligible bachelor in the Agrawal community, six feet one, quite good looking according to mirror reports- here he was mooning after a girl who had rejected him, in a love sick, Hindi movie- hero type fashion! Shame!

Next day he gave the car keys to his mother saying that he did not need it, but it was all his mother's fault that he had to go out- she wanted to go to the temple. He took her, grumbling and as they were passing the main market, he saw her with an older version of herself- and the younger sister; this must be the mother! He had no idea that he had stopped the car and was watching the trio dazedly. The mother was good looking, no wonder the daughters were so. Suddenly the younger sister saw him, smiled impishly and said something to the mother, and the lady turned and looked at him directly. He froze. Would she create a row? She looked the sort who would not hesitate in boxing a fellow's ears if it was necessary, but she was persuaded by 'Her" to enter a shop.

The car keys were with his mother so Rohit spent the next morning in scolding the servants, complaining about the food, the weather, his sister's and father's behavior. Then he had nothing to do. It was raining very hard, but he thought he could go for a drive, he assuaged his conscience by telling himself that "She" wouldn't venture in such weather. He again took the turn past the college merely because the road was better that side, he told himself. Naturally she was there.

The rain water reached her knees, there was no rickshaw in sight, she was holding her books in one hand and the umbrella with the other and was wading slowly. Ah! What an opportunity! He drove to her side and opening the door said, "Do sit down, I will drop you home."

"No thank you." Progressing mate? At least she had spoken.

"Please, please, how can you go home like this?"

"That won't be necessary." such cool words. He blurted out "Just cut it out, will you? Its raining so hard, you are wet and I must see you home."

"That won't be necessary." The tone was stern now. God knows what happened to him then, he should have acted with more restraint but he couldn't help it. Standing in the rain he grabbed her hands and said, "Urvashi, I love you." Later on he felt that it was the most foolish thing that he could have said and in a most foolish manner, rather Bollywood movie fashion, but even the setting was Hindi movie type- the rain, the flooded streets, their being alone (barring the presence of a traffic policeman who was watching them with great enthusiasm).

Her eyes blazed. She pulled her hands away saying, "I knew you were that sort. Don't come after me again." He saw her walking away and felt physical pain. He remembered driving slowly after her till she found a vehicle. He saw that she reached home safely and went home.

Home was pandemonium. His father had had a massive heart attack, he was being searched for frantically and by the time he reached his father's side, the old tycoon had passed away. It was all so sudden. The responsibilities that fell on his shoulders were heavier than he had imagined. The old man had his fingers in so many pies and it all fell on him. By the time he had recovered, things had changed. He went to the yellow house to seriously talk with her grandfather and get her parents' address but there was a lock. She had gone to Delhi for further studies and the old couple had gone to stay with their son. He even went to Delhi and roamed the streets near the university, no, he did not see her again.

Time passed, he bowed to maternal pressure and married the Tibrewala girl. Life changed, he changed and so did his values; and at this stage Rohit Agrawal felt that the old Rohit was totally alien from the old one, except in her matter. He had come too far to retrace his steps. But his Enigma, his search for her was the only unchanging thing about him. Maybe, with more time, her memory might fade but it would never go away- her cool and peaceful look and the words that he would never understand, "That won't be necessary."

THREE

Kaleidoscope

Nineteen hundred and twenty:

Yogmaya lifted her head and listened intently. Apart from the thumping sound made by the pestles that were pounding paddy, she thought that she could hear a familiar voice. But she did not- the large verandah where the men folk sat and the guests were entertained, was at a distance- not much could be heard in this noise. She wiped her forehead with the corner of her coarse saree and began pounding again. She must have imagined the voice. It was so long that she had not seen her parents; she counted the years, four years before her daughter was born, that made it fourteen years. Fourteen years since she saw her parents! Her father-in-law had harbored some grievances against her father, mainly about some cattle not given in dowry, and so, festival after festival went, and messenger after messenger was sent away. Yogmaya could not go home.

She heard a shrill voice shout, "Don't take all day- there is so much to do", it was her mother-in-law. She bent over the paddy again, but as soon as the old lady's back was turned, her youngest sister-in-law ran to her and whispered, "The barber from your home has come!" Yogmaya's heart lifted, barbers in those times were also used as messengers, may be this time her father-in-law would relent and let her go home. She mentally offered a mound of paddy to the Kali temple if she were allowed to go.

"No, no this is not possible" she heard her father-in-law say to someone. And feeding the fire in the mud oven, Yogmaya's hand stopped mid way. What! Would they refuse again! What sort of heartlessness was this? Leaving the oven untended, she rushed t o the inner courtyard where her mother-in-law sat and fell on her feet weeping, "O ma, ma, please let me go this time," she sobbed. For a second the old one's heart softened and though there was curtness in her tone, the concern was evident, "Go, tend the cooking. I will see what I can do."

As the mustard seeds spluttered, she put the chopped ribbed gourd in the Karahi and through the noise heard the softened, pleading tones of her mother-in-law; the tone that she especially reserved for her husband. Snatches of conversation floated through the air," That old man is dying, it will be a sin if we don't send her now."

"And what about his promises?"

"Leave it- that was such a long time back- moreover the girl works so hard."

"This is the harvesting season, should we send her?" Then there was silence, Yogmaya waited with bated breath, "We will send you after the harvest is over." The words fell like a blow-suppose her father died. In an imploring tone Yogmaya asked, "What news is there of my parents?" Without flinching once the old lady said, "O, they are all right."

Noiselessly the tears fell as she patted the thick corn rotis in shape and slowly toasted them. She knew she would never see her father again. Oh, why did God make her a woman, worse than cattle, for cattle had no feelings, no memories and just like the monsoon rain Yogmaya's tears fell thick and fast. Her daughter, Gayatri came in, all of ten years old already, showing signs of great beauty. The men folk were talking about her marriage. She wiped her mother's tears and started patting the corn rotis to shape. "Don't cry, ma, we will find a way." She said, knowing that no way could be found that her mother could see her father.

At night when she was gently massaging her husband's feet, she found him unusually caring, asking about the jewellery that she would like on the next festival. Then he cleared his throat, "It is said that a man who has no son cannot attain moksha". Yogmaya decided to keep quiet. "So father decided that I should marry again." Yogmaya kept quiet. "The girl is from Rajnagar, she can read and write. The marriage is next month." Yogmaya did not break her silence, only the grip on his feet became stronger. "You will be respected more as you are the elder."

A sob escaped her and her whole body shuddered with grief. What she was fearing all these days had come true! Ah! It was the fate of a woman!

Nineteen hundred and forty five:

The cold north wind swept back his thick, black hair as he stood on the edge of the long verandah, arms across his chest. The Inquisitors sat in front, they comprised of his grandfather, father and various uncles. The tinkle of cowbells reminded him that dusk was approaching. "So, you have decided to act upon your wishes?" this was his grandfather, the stern voice could not be anyone else's. He thought it better not to reply, and as was fitting, kept his eyes on the ground. "We are spending so much on his education, giving him the best, and look at his ingratitude!" the high pitch belonged to his father. "Some decision has to be taken today", elder uncle's voice was firm.

Yes, the decision was already taken; it was merely to be put before the Inquisition. His wife had not produced a son, daughter upon daughter followed; then there was a long gap. The elders thought it most essential that he marry again- not for himself but for the family name- he being the only son amongst all the uncles. First coaxing and cajoling was done and the bait of extremely beautiful girls and large tracts of land was dangled before him. Thinking that his wife's presence was hindering his compliance, they sent her away for a visit to her father's home. His solitude made most members of the family coax him for the marriage, "Who will send us water through tarpan on shraddh days if there is no son?" they lamented.

But he was adamant- none but Gayatri would be his wife-it was not her fault that she did not bear sons, God had other plans. Then came the threats- for he was doing his M.A in English Literature from a famous college in a far away city. "Your allowances stop the day you refuse." Grand pa's threat. "You shall not receive an inch of property". Father's threats. "You will have to leave home." Elder Uncle's warning.

He thought deeply about everything and the lines of Kipling's poem "IF" came to him. All right, even after losing all he would re-build. The way would be thorny but he would never marry again. He was brought back to the present by a lone voice pleading his case- it was his youngest uncle- a man forced to marry twice. "Take my example- from the day I married again I have had no peace- do not force the boy." This was quashed promptly by the growls that rose against him. So, the battle was lost!. "Speak" shrieked his father "Yes or no" All eyes were turned in his direction. His reed- like body stood straight and firm with strong determination. He looked at them and said, "No."

Immediately a furor arose as each vied to heap on him the choicest of curses. Through their shouts he heard his grandfather's voice, the cold fury in it ready to slice through him, "Leave tomorrow. "Tomorrow? Why tomorrow? Leave today and now, not a moment will you stay here and defile my house, you infilial wretch!" This rage was his father's.

He found himself going to the inner courtyard where the women folk sat with bated breath- sympathy written large on the faces of all. As his own mother had died when he was a baby and his stepmother a real step, so he turned to his grandmother who sat sobbing. "I leave now," he said. "O my child, my motherless child!" and she wrapped her arms around him, unwilling to let him go. His tear- filled eyes took in for the last time the large courtyard, the tulsi in the center and the women pounding the paddy. He would not see it again- may be if his mother had lived, things would have been different, he consoled himself.

As reality dawned on the old lady, she noticed the thin outer garments of the boy and ran in to get a warm shawl. Like a person gone berserk her eyes swept the place to give him something to eat before he left. She saw the freshly pounded pressed rice and the jaggery that had been taken out from the moulds and put handfuls of the pressed rice in a sari of hers that was drying with a few wedges of jaggery and handed it to the boy, tears raining down her cheeks, preventing any further speech.

The boy left home and walked briskly to an unknown destination- his heart satisfied that justice was done. So Yogmaya's daughter Gayatri was spared the misery of having a rival at home.

Nineteen hundred and seventy five:

The large crowd in the outpatient's department of the government hospital seemed to grow longer and longer and the noise seemed to get unbearable with the heat. Dr. Mira looked at her watch, four hours had passed and still so many were left! The letter on her table bothered her. The clear and well formed writing on the envelope was her father's. She was greatly tempted to take it out and read it ignoring the crowd, but no, it would not do. She stood up to stretch and saw the long line of hopefuls outside waiting for admission to the Medical College next door. Was it not only yesterday that she too was in that line, starry eyed, accompanied by her husband?

She had been married at a very tender age, fourteen to be precise, a brilliant student but her husband understood her need to study further. "What are your subjects?" he had asked her. "Physics, Chemistry and Biology" she had whispered through tears unshed. "But why do you cry?" the compassion in his voice was a thing to be felt. "Because

I will never study again." And the hot tears fell "Of course you will, as long as you like."

His promise was not empty; his presence being everywhere it was needed. And what a rock of Gibraltar had been his mother! Realizing her daughter-in-law's desire and potential she threw in her whole hearted support. Gossiping friends would incite her, "Whoever thought of educating a daughter-in-law!" said one. "Who will do the house work?" said another. To all that the crusty old lady gave a fitting reply and the sharpness of her tongue ended all queries.

The years of struggle were hard but fulfilling and then through her hard work and innate brilliance she became a very qualified and successful doctor, first working for the government then starting a nursing home of her own. She specialized in Gynaecology, her own special way to come to the aid of her own kind. She preferred to work in the villages and soon became a Florence Nightingale for them. Pitiful cases of Womanhood would come her way- most of the ailments and diseases contracted were due to lack of education, awareness and basic sanitation.

The cup of tea lay cold on her table as she read the letter again and again. The words seemed to resound in her ears and seemed etched in her brain, "So your mother's condition is finally diagnosed by the doctors as Alzheimer's. It is a great shock to me and I feel helpless. I cannot look after her myself anymore, suggest a place where they look after such patients." Mira was aghast! Her mother and Alzheimer's! It could not be! Tears of sorrow blinded her as she took up paper and pen. "… and we have decided that Ma will stay with us and be looked after by us, no other."

"But how can we stay with a daughter?" her father had asked. "It is because being a doctor I can look after my mother in the best possible way and because your son-in-law loves her too." She had replied. "Apart from care my mother needs love." And then they had moved to her home and stayed there. A retinue of maids was appointed for her mother's care. Mira who had tended her mother-in-law suffering from Parkinson's disease would now tend to her mother.

So Yogmaya's grand daughter, Gayatri's daughter Mira, took the onus of looking after her parents.

Two Thousand Two:

Tension lay thickly everywhere. Policemen with riot equipment stood poised to countermand any attack. Ishani Mishra, S.P, Godhra, paced up and down the street with the men. Communal violence had erupted as suddenly and viciously as a dormant volcano. Ishani was determined that there would be no loss of life in her area. Constant supervision, open mind and excellent rapport with her subordinate was paying dividends. All of a sudden she stiffened and whirled, in the far darkness a point of light appeared and as soon was extinguished. That was enough. "Charge" she commanded just as hundreds of men screaming dementedly appeared from nowhere. Some fled, some were bundled away while up and down she paced the streets appealing for peace on her speaker. The radio in her Gypsy crackled- it was the DG, "Any casualties?" "None sir," she said proudly. "Good" he commended. She smiled wryly – good indeed.

What trials and tribulations she had gone through to hear those words! What lengths she had to go to convince her superiors that she could beat the men around her in any sort of combat! Where she lacked in physique, she made up with pre-planning, surprise and much extra work. It was not that the gender increased or decreased anyone's capacity—it was the zeal with which it was accomplished. She spared no one—least of all herself.

Thus, Yogmaya's great grand daughter, Gayatri's grand-daughter and Mira's daughter showed to the world what stuff a woman is made of.

FOUR

The Full Circle

Dr. Neelam Joshi was in her clinic and in a militant mood. The senior nurse had demanded another raise in her salary and this time the demand disguised a veiled threat -- unless complied with, she would move to greener pastures. Greener pastures indeed! From the time the Sarala Nursing Home had been set up right across the road, her problems had begun. They offered their staff a better salary so she had to give her own staff increments; then the problem with patients. Some of her regulars started showing up there too and in no way could she prevent it. And now this, Sapna Saha was a very good nurse and quite indispensable, and she knew it.

Just then the cause of her present wrath appeared near the door way, "A special case Madam," and in came a middle aged couple with a very pretty girl. It looked as if the girl had been weeping for hours. Her face was puffy, eyes blood shot and even her lips were swollen. Dr. Joshi guessed the problem even before anyone had opened their mouths- she had been in this game for two decades now, "Yes?" she asked brusquely., she did not believe in bedside manners. The man tried to speak, then motioned towards the girl, clearing his throat. "She is pregnant; has to be aborted." Yes she had guessed correctly. The same old game; pretty daughter, sordid love affair, pregnancy, coming to a small town, unknown place to get rid of it in anonymity.

"How many months?"

"Seven"

Dr. Neelam Joshi nearly shot out of her seat. She had a powerful voice and she turned it full blast on them. "What were you doing till now? At seven months you ask for an abortion? The baby is full grown now, who will take the risk? Wait for two months and have it delivered, then if you do not want it leave it in an orphanage."

The mother spoke now-"She was in a hostel so we did not know- the abortion has to be done- she is getting married next week."

So they were going to dupe some innocent fellow. This is the stuff out of which our righteous high class is made of. Thank goodness she never married! No man was worth the trouble. And she had seen too many ungrateful children to ever wish having her own.

She viewed the case clinically. Yes if she could inject that drug then the girl would go into labour and whatever it was would be ejected. She could manage it- if she did not then the doctor at Sarala Nursing Home would take it up readily. "Prepare the O.T and prepare her." She pointed at the girl as if she were scum.

She had known it would be a difficult case, but that it was nearly going to cost her, her medical reputation she had not foreseen. The girl was losing a lot of blood and the most unfortunate thing about it was that Dr. Neelam Joshi, MBBS, MS, FRCOG became nervous. Truly catastrophic! The arrogant doctor of the hated nursing home had to be summoned and together they had brought the girl away from the brink of death. Amidst all this confusion and chaos, all had forgotten the cause of grief- the little baby. Too big for a seven month baby, it looked quite healthy and happy and lay quite contentedly on the table where the head nurse had dumped it. Its black eyes looked on quietly.

The girl lay limply and the mother fussed over her and the father came to her from time to time to give something to make her more comfortable. The nurses flitted around, each outdoing the other in showing service-they had found out that the patient was a very rich person and the very rich leave large tips. In that hustle bustle entered Dr. Joshi after having refreshed herself with a cup of tea and a fresh, crisp, cotton saree. She looked at all the fuss for the foolish girl who should have been made to bear the consequences instead of being pampered, and then saw the baby lying quietly on the table. Her heart went out to the little bundle who should have been pampered and fussed over but due to a quirk of fate lay uncared for. She took the bundle in her arms and the baby opened its eyes and looked at her solemnly and smiled. The old doctor felt a rush of love for the brave infant that would not die despite all the methods used to destroy it. "You will stay with me," she whispered to the baby.

After four days the girl left the clinic without once asking for the baby- the parents did not even bother to see it. All they wanted was some medicine that would dry up the milk that had formed in the girl's breasts. That would be a tell tale sign and so it had to be removed. Dr. Joshi wearily wrote out a prescription and was glad to see them go.

Years went by, other places prospered and grew but that small, sleepy place remained what it was and soon the incident was forgotten.

Thirty years hence:

The Chief Minister looked at her watch and then at the door. Rehana should have come by now. How she waited for her daughter's arrival every three months! It was such a wrench to her heart when she had allowed the child to take up her studies at the London School of Economics, but how could one curb the talent of one's child for one's own needs? And that for such a gifted one as Rehana was. She had always tried not to be over indulgent with her, after all, she had to be trained to take over the empire after her as she had done after the untimely demise of her husband.

She remembered what a naive, jittery fool she had been when she was married; and what a suave, polished, debonair person her husband had been. There was no comparison to be made- she was a student and he was the State Minister of Education. It was in their college function that he had seen her, talked to her and sent a marriage proposal to her parents for her. Oh, he knew how to go through the proper channel wherever it mattered. After marriage he groomed her for politics, "When I am CM, I want you to be in my cabinet," he would tell her whenever she would not want to go on the extensive tours of canvassing and propaganda for the party. So, she went unwillingly at first but soon she started enjoying it all and he did not have to persuade her. They said her beauty fetched the crowds but, the spiteful Opposition, were all wrong. He was so good looking, so charming that people came just to see him and he was also a powerful orator. You have to be good in histrionics to enter the political arena, she realized as she had seen the many moods and faces of her husband. One moment he would be the dear son of an old peasant woman in the crowd, and the other moment an affectionate brother to some village oaf, who would have his back patted and would go away gloating. And as for the young women- his charm oozed and he had just the right words and the right manner for them and many a girl left starry eyed. Initially she had been quite jealous but soon she realized that it was his modus operandi and it ceased to bother her.

Naturally he became the CM, there was no one else better than him to fill the post. She was not a member of his cabinet- she was still too raw and needed exposure, he said.

Those were the days! She had known the luxury of money earlier but she had not tasted from the goblet of power and it was a heady intoxicant. The best part of it was that she got all the roses without having to face the thorns for she was his wife, and as all know, the CM's wife is more important than he is. The bowing and scraping of even the rich and influential, the adulation of the masses, the fear in the eyes of officials fearing her displeasure, the parting of crowds, the hushed voices, what new sense of pleasure was she developing that she enjoyed them so much? She did not have to face the brick bats from the opposition, she did not have to answer for each and every action that turned out unfortunate, she had merely the rosy side of it, her husband laughingly said.

But she was always with him so she learned his game fast. Apart from being a good politician, he was a very loving and understanding husband and after their daughter was born, a loving father too. Yes, he was too young to be the CM but he proved to be a better statesman than the doddering old fogies and so he was elected for a second term. This time she was in his cabinet- Information and Broadcasting.

Just when the world seemed paradise and even the Everest seemed quite approachable, he had to die in that plane crash. She did not have any last words, any parting advice, anything at all that would keep her going. She felt she was in a void, alone, defenseless. It was in such despondence when she was sitting in her office looking at files without reading them, when unannounced, the Finance Minister walked in. She was quite surprised. He was the biggest contender to the "throne" and she was "the widow", the contenders were quite wary of her.

After the usual formalities of enquiring about health, and her daughter, he came straight to the point. "The party feels that you should take up the reins now." She listened aghast- she? How could she run this turbulent state? What did she know of politics? She was completely broken, devastated. He had answers to all that. She was chosen, as honestly, she was his widow. His charisma was such that in-fighting in the party would not take place and so it would be stronger. Elections were nearing and the party image had to be considered.

She had accepted and her husband's grooming had helped her tremendously. She slipped in the role efficiently and was doing commendable work too, but the home front was quite neglected and Rehana had to be sent to a boarding school.

The next elections came and she won a place for herself again, and she was known in her own right as a politician, no more merely as his widow. With the passage of time she changed, matured, took up challenges easily and started defeating people in their own game. It was a world of cut throat competition where survival was only possible if one was forever wary. She had a clean image- she took occasional gifts- that came with the office and had a drink or two but in the privacy of her bedroom. Khadi and cognac did not mix. The flesh longed at times for satiation which could be found if she gave the slightest of signs, but no, the risk was too great, moreover she had Rehana to think of.

A woman with sons can afford to have affairs, she felt, but a woman with daughters cannot. The influence would be too damaging. She still wore lacy underwear beneath her coarse khadi. Sometimes, while removing them at night, she would look at them and smile ruefully- for whom? The Finance Minister- he was again FM in her cabinet- was still a bachelor. When he came for discussion on state matters, there were a couple of occasions when they were alone. She would be very aware of his maleness, his cologne and the message in his eyes which he would try to conceal. Once, while going over some data, their fingers had touched and the effect was electric- he had kept on looking at her with parted lips and she had half- willed those lips to fall on hers when the secretary came with tea and the spell was broken. They could not look each other in the eye many days afterwards. Maybe, one day, after she retired from politics.

She heard the car door slam and as she rose, Rehana came into the room. She sensed the depression in her daughter just as she kissed her but decided not to say anything just then- there were too many servants about. Dinner was a quiet affair and Rehana hardly ate anything. It was in the privacy of the bedroom that the girl broke down. "O Mama I was raped!". She could not believe her ears at first and when the words really sank in, she was livid with rage! She, Chinmoyee Devi, one of the most powerful women in the country, she had to hear that her daughter was raped! All right she would make the animal regret the day he was born.

"Who was he? I will first have him castrated and then we will deal with him."

"Mama, I don't know. He was some sort of a maniac who had raped other girls of the locality also and the police haven't caught him yet. But Oh Mum, the worst part is this- I'm pregnant."

Her world turned dark as she heard this; the CM in her surfaced. The opposition just had to get this and would turn it to a spicy story to titillate the masses- and the image of the party would suffer! Had she been an ordinary woman, she would have her daughter aborted quietly, but in her place, even a walk on the beach made news. What could she do? Who to turn to? She longed for her husband's presence and after a long time felt utterly helpless. What to do next, she wondered.

Then she thought of the FM. He had always been her ally- he had given up his chance to be CM just because the party would be strengthened, would he not help her now? Yes, he would be the right person to turn to. She phoned him and he came immediately. He took over just as he used to whenever she felt like giving up. There was a clinic at Warisnagar, six hours from there- very small, but the private clinic was run by a reputed gynaecologist. They could take

Rehana there and the matter would be over soon. The doctor was a party member and would surely keep the matter to herself; moreover, nobody would dare cross the CM!

She sighed with relief. Yes, he had come to her side when she needed him most- a true friend indeed! Next day they left early, separately in their personal cars. All appointments were cancelled- she did not know what excuse the FM gave to his office, she only knew that it would be a good one. Rehana was quiet the whole way, and when her mother asked her why she did not have this matter finished in London, she said that she had been too afraid. Poor fatherless girl- her heart went out to her daughter- why did she have to suffer?

Warisnagar proved to be small and sleepy as they had heard of it. Apart from a few shops from which blaring film music cut the silence, there was little else to be noticed, and they soon reached the clinic. It was a sort of nursing home, very small but very clean. The nurse took them in. The doctor was a slip of a girl who no way looked as if she had earned all those degrees-MBBS, MS, FRCOG, a Shraddha Joshi.

"Yes?"

She was roused out of her thoughts but before she could answer, the FM spoke up.

"Our daughter has to be aborted."

"How many months?" her tone was matter of fact, no questioning, no disapproval, no patronizing.

"Two"

"It will cost you four hundred and fifty rupees and whatever else the medicines come to. Nurse, prepare the patient."

Rehana was taken in and she was left to wander around the place. The FM had left, he did not think it wise that he stay there too long. The waiting room seemed familiar, had she seen it somewhere? Utter foolishness! How could it ever be so?

She sat again on the hard chair and started flipping through a magazine- she could not concentrate. She wanted the business to be over as soon as possible. And just then an old lady in a wheel chair came in, her entry so noiseless that none was aware of her presence, but there she was- fat, bespectacled, with a lot of grey hair.

"I see you come again."

"I beg your pardon, there must be some mistake, this is the first time I have come here." She was irritated, why couldn't she be left alone! Her hand automatically reached for the bell that would summon the orderly to remove the unwanted presence- but oh, she was not in her office.

"You came here thirty years ago for an abortion. Yours is a face one does not forget easily, and so I followed your career. Quite spectacular- deserves congratulations."

"Who are you?" she could barely whisper. So, the matter had not been forgotten-it had buried itself so well in the recesses of her brain that she had ceased to think of it and now this old hag, this odious creature, was reminding her of her past folly! Yes, she remembered now. No wonder the place looked so familiar! She was engulfed by a wave of memories, the terror she had experienced, the way her parents had looked after her, the pain; and now her daughter was going through the same torture. Strange are your ways, Maker. In the haze of pain and the stupor of medicines she had not realized what was happening to her or around her.

Her parents were frantic with worry lest the marriage be called off with that extremely eligible minister, but for her, only the pain and the shame existed.

They had given her medicines to stop the flow of milk- and her milk dried up completely, it did not come out even when Rehana was born; motherhood being punished. Her husband had been very kind and understanding when she told him (as she was coached) that she had been very ill so the marriage was consummated only after she was fit. Sometimes she wondered if he had known- but even if he had, he never let her know it.

But there was a baby too. Her mother said it was dead and she had asked if it was a boy or girl and her mother had roughly told her that she had not bothered to find out. Well, she might as well do it now.

"You're the doctor, aren't you?" she asked. The old woman nodded. "What did I deliver?" she knew it was folly to ask but suddenly it seemed so important for her to know. "Was it a boy or a girl?"

"Girl"

"Where did you bury her?"

"Why would we have done so? She was a very healthy baby, who was a very good girl and who is now a very good doctor- the one you have met."

The cool girl-doctor came in just then-"Madam you can leave, it is over."

And Chinmoyee Devi, Chief Minister, looked up and saw her daughter, the one she had unknowingly abandoned thirty years ago.

Life had come to a full circle.

FIVE

The Debt

Mrs. Srivastava looked at the house critically, "Quite all right," she told her husband-only it looks so old and is so isolated." "Do we have to live here,?" the patient Mr. Srivastava exploded suddenly, "Manya, you have rejected dozens of houses by now- be sure you can't get anymore and the wedding is just a week away." So they agreed that the old house would be the place where they would hold the marriage of their daughter. The Srivastavas were from Allahabad but the groom's family was from Kota and it was on their request that the marriage was to be held in Kota and so ensued a hectic house hunting. The houses they had seen were either too small or too old or too close to the next house and so the finicky Mrs. Srivastava had rejected one house after the other. After all it was their only daughter's wedding. And at last they chanced upon this house.

The house stood alone in that lane, grey, double storied and majestic- the wide windows and spacious balconies speaking of times when land was plentiful. The garden was overgrown with weeds and other such plants that are quick to smother the civilized plants and Mrs. Srivastava made a quick note- first have the garden cleared.

At last the house was clean. The owners were very generous- they lived abroad and an old uncle had the key. “If you repair and paint the place and tidy the garden then you don’t have to pay rent” he said. The Srivastavas were delighted- after all they had only to stay a week in the house but despite it, the gesture was generous. The house sparkled and had a warmth and joy about it that is seen in the ambience of old houses which are forgotten and set aside from ones attention but when suddenly they get love and care and attention, they are rejuvenated.

Only two days were left for the wedding and the whole house was in turmoil-smothered with relatives, she felt from her side, from her husband’s side. Songs, merry laughter, shouts, jokes echoed in those large rooms and despite the hard work, all of it was such great fun. Mrs. Srivastava put the jewelry back in the steel cupboard- she had just stacked all the expensive sarees there-tomorrow they would pack it. It was past midnight and her bones were weary from the toil of the day. The bed looked inviting and she dropped off.

“Ma, O Ma”, “Ma, O Ma”, who was calling out? Her own Shruti always called her mummy; she tried to rub the sleep away from her eyes and woke up groggily- the luminous dial of the wrist watch indicated that it was two in the night- had she fallen asleep here? She sat up and with a pounding of her heart saw that the cupboard was wide open. “Divine mother! Don’t let me hear that we have been robbed!” she muttered and just then stood thunder struck, immobile.

A very beautiful girl, hardly eighteen, stood near the cupboard trying on the jewels, draping the saree around her. At first glance, she wondered if it was Meeta, her niece, but why would she do such a thing? The girl came closer. "Ma, Ma, why did you desert me?"

Mrs. Srivastava trembled with fright-"Who are you" she asked.

"Ma, you don't remember, I do. In your last birth you were my mother and you died when I was small. Father married again and this was our house. I was to be married when I was eighteen and father had bought so much jewelry for me that my step-mother was furious and just two days before my wedding had me poisoned. So there was no wedding for me and I started living here. Then when I saw you here, I knew that my release has come. O Ma, the groom you have chosen for your daughter, in previous birth was supposed to be mine!"

Mrs. Srivastava clutched the sheets with fear. Her first thought was to run to her husband and call him. He always sorted out her problems- today he would solve this too. The spirit sensed this.

"Don't be afraid Ma, I am your daughter but don't tell anyone about me otherwise they will send me away again and I will never be released."

"What release do you talk of?" Mrs. Srivastava asked.

"My soul wanders aimlessly in these halls because I waited for my true love here and before I could be rightfully his, I was killed. If he accepts me once more, I will be released." the spirit said.

Mrs. Srivastava was aghast. What was this girl talking of? Now, when she looked at her closely, she looked merely like a beautiful girl- was somebody trying to hood wink her? Her practical sense prevailed and soon she was in control of her senses.

"First put away the sarees and the jewelry- I don't want any nosy relative snooping in and concocting stories- then tell me what I must do." She said.

The girl- spirit did as bidden and then sat beside her. What a lovely pink complexion and such long black hair! Mrs. Srivastava was proud of her own daughter's beauty but this girl made her feel prouder- she had only begotten beauties!

"When your son-in-law comes to wed, then before he puts sindoor in the hair parting of your daughter, he must put it on mine- that will give me the peace I seek and I will be released from this endless waiting."

Amarendra, her handsome, debonair neurosurgeon son-in-law, how could she tell him so and moreover, even if she did, would he listen, would anyone believe what she was hearing? They would call her mad and may be even cancel the marriage. It had taken so much time and patience to have fixed this negotiation and now, this problem.

But was this girl a problem? The mother in Mrs. Srivastava awoke in defence, a spirit will not lie- she must have been the girl's mother. If she had died and the child had gone through so much pain, did she not owe this to the girl?

"But what do I tell all the people about you? And you know these times- the groom might not agree- Shruti might throw tantrums."

"Ma, you loved me so much once." If a spirit could have tears in her eyes- the eyes of the girl filled. Instinctively, she put out her hands to take the girl's hands in hers to comfort her, but the girl drew back, "you must not touch me."

"What do I have to do Child?" "Nothing much. When the groom takes the pinch of sindoor, just instruct him to put it behind your daughter's head first and then on your daughter. I will sit so close to her that the sindoor will fall on my parting."

"But what do I tell the others who you are?"

"Not to worry- apart from you no one else will be able to see me."

Just then the tower clock in the town struck four and a cock started crowing somewhere. "I have to leave Ma- I will come again tomorrow- then tell me what you have thought."

The sun rose and a flurry of activity began. "Why did you sleep in the corner room Bhabhi, we were all waiting for you here" her sister-in-law asked as she served tea. Mrs. Srivastava was glad that just as the relatives had started arriving she had assigned their jobs to them and her own workload was shared. Her elder sister-in-law looked after the food and so she had come with the servant bearing the tray.

"I must have dropped off- I was so tired," she replied.

Shruti came in – radiant and snuggled up to her mother. Mrs. Srivastava ran her fingers through her daughter's short hair and remembered the silky tresses of the one whom no one could see.

"Mummy, mummy" Shruti called out- but why did Mrs. Srivastava's ears echo with the "Ma, O Ma"?

In the evening Amarendra arrived with his friends- she highly disapproved of it but these were modern times and he had to go abroad just after marriage so she did not say anything. "They are to be married next day so why do you object?" her husband had counseled. But Amarendra was highly educated and his excellent manners and behavior banished all misgivings she had about his modern ways. The evening was a success and even she had enjoyed it-for the boys and girls had danced and sang and all had joined in and there was much merry making.

As they were leaving- Amarendra looked all around- "What are you searching for?" Mrs. Srivastava had asked. "The juhi creeper- from the time I have come I have been surrounded by its scent, wonder where it is."

There was no juhi creeper but Mrs. Srivastava knew where the fragrance came from- the girl was with him all the time! The same fragrance surrounded her at night when they were talking.

Late at night she came into the corner room who knows what the girl-spirit might do, if she did not go and assure her that what she desired would be done? After all, she would tell Amarendra it was an old custom and no one would be the wiser. The girl was there, and was smiling happily.

"I had so much fun ma- I too danced."

"I did not see you. Can you dance?"

"Yes, after you died, Father took very good care of me and had appointed tutors to teach me dance and music. I can sing well too."

And mother and daughter chatted- time stood still, the barrier between the ages vanished; spirit and human seemed to lose their fear of each other as they united. Both knew that it was the last time that they were talking. The girl-spirit would leave the next night.

"And will you be happy after that my child?" she had asked.

"Forever, Ma, forever." She had said.

The wedding day was a day to remember and she felt that there were wings to her feet. But should she not tell her husband all that she was experiencing? Did she ever hide anything from him, ever? So drawing him in the backyard she told him all that had taken place.

He grew quiet as he listened and then said, "you owe her this- but be careful nobody even hears of this."

The wedding band could be heard and the waves of music brought joy to all the hearts. The ancient house was decked out in splendor- tiny bulbs fitted to all the jutting eaves and parapets. The garden was more a fairy land with twinkling lights sparkling from the trees and bushes. And when Mr. and Mrs. Srivastava saw the groom their hearts burst with pride- though modern he had thought it fit to wear the traditional dhoti-kurta to the wedding- and their Shruti looked like a fairy- a goddess. The time for the "sindoordan" began and the ladies started singing the song sung during the occasion.

A strong fragrance of juhi wafted in the air as Mrs. Srivastava asked Amarendra to put some sindoor behind Shruti first. "But this is not done," protested her mother-in-law.

"It will be done from now on" insisted Mrs. Srivastava. The sindoor was first put there, then on Shruti's parting.

A strong gust of wind blew, the fragrance of juhi became stronger and then wafted away. Mrs. Srivastava felt something cold touch her cheeks and something whispered and went by; a grateful daughter's kiss? a grateful girl-spirit's good bye?

SIX

The Victory

Varsha Chauhan took another puff at her cigarette, the smoke that she blew out went directly over the face of the old party worker who tried to cloak his disgust by bending down to pick a piece of paper. The map of Himmatnagar and its adjoining villages lay spread on the table and she was marking the canvassing process with a red pencil. The pencil line streaked through various villages and came to a stop near Viratpur. "We have to strengthen our forces here-Viratpur may prove to be my Waterloo-", "Need not worry, Rani Sahiba," fawned a supporter, "You will win everywhere."

"Yes, Rani sahiba, the old Maharajah Saheb's name was enough for the people to vote for his party, you won the last elections, why do you worry?" This was a worker who had changed parties some time back. She was never sure of his intentions, but he was a good orator and proved invaluable in the canvassing.

Two months of sheer labor, brow beating, anticipating the moves of the enemy and planning the counter-attack, which general could outwit her tactics? But generals had their superiors, their governments to back them, their armies to follow each instruction, but for her? The high ups in the party disapproved of her clean ways- she would not take money- this put them back for their image was sullied so there was opposition from that front. The opposition was stalking each move of hers just waiting for the wrong one to tear her apart. And her own supporters? What irony! She knew that they were mercenaries, that if the opposition offered them much more they'd turn against her, not all, most of them, most were drunken sods who'd start a brawl at the drop of a hat! Yes, some were there, who were faithful to the royal family and put in selfless service and it was on them that she banked upon. But the back breaking, feet wearing work of canvassing! No matter how much you did for the villages, they always had plenty of grievances.

Buses were infrequent and late, the schools did not run properly, no drinking water, and it went on and on. She wanted to laugh at the way the tables had turned. When she was a little girl these people had such a fawning attitude, such a servile way but now she had to do the fawning, it was she who was servile! Times had changed. Education and opportunity had lifted them so high that they considered themselves on par with her! She remembered with distaste how she had nearly bickered with a farmer's son who alleged that she had set up a farm just to benefit her own workers not the villagers!

Was it worth it? She would ask herself time and again. She could live in as leisurely way as she desired, she had so many hobbies, had her precious dogs to look after, her huge gardens were being neglected, oh, was it worth it? If she could just shrug it off and walk away from it all, what bliss would it be! She glanced at the photograph on the opposite wall and the Maharaja's eyes seemed to bore her through and through. "Go ahead, leave it all, daughter, you were a weak escapist, prove it to them." She turned back guiltily from her thoughts and took up Viratnagar again.

The campaigning was being done efficiently- the reports she got from her sources said so. She herself had done a whirl wind round of the town and villages once and now she was touring a second time, slowly, patiently listening to the problems, not showing her irritation and anger when some in the crowd jeered and asked where she was all the five years when she was in power, (all such sent by the Opposition no doubt, her supporters assured) even wearing the sort of prints and material the village folk wore, making a point to eat her mid-day meal with some villagers, the food being cooked by some loyal supporters- the same staple diet day in and day out- thick "makki rotis" and some curry. She did not mind the food, often did not notice what she ate, it was all so unimportant.

The days seemed to pass in a haze- the same routine repeated over and over again- get up at five, have a hurried bath, dress, feed the dogs (they would not eat unless she fed them) swallow a morsel or two of whatever her servants placed before her and go to her office in her Gypsy. There her party workers would be waiting; they'd all assemble and then walk- thanks to the Chief Election Commissioner! The entire day she'd spend in walking and talking, walking till her soles seemed to wear off, talking till her jaws ached. Constant smiling made her cheek muscles sore.

They'd reassemble at her office around nine p.m and plan the next day's work- that would take two hours. She'd reach home, have the one luxury she waited for- a long soaking in the tub, eat and it would be around one before she would get to sleep and she would have just turned around in bed when Veera, her personal maid would awaken her. Well, she should not complain, she had chosen it.

Ten days before election she got the news that her rival in the Opposition had just got enormous funds to distribute among the tribals. Then his plan was to have oath-taking ceremonies- once the tribals swore on a pile of grain they would remain true to their word and would vote only for him. Disaster! She knew how gullible they were! All her efforts would go in vain! What could be done?

Suggestions poured forth from each direction- some too foolish, some violent, some that would line the pockets of those who suggested. She listened quietly and took a decision, a fateful decision- that money would not be distributed- she would see to it. She would prevent this usurper from trying to take away the throne that rightfully belonged to her, and she made plans.

Each night her party men scoured the villages and whenever they encountered the vehicles of the Opposition, fights would ensue- sometimes verbal, sometimes violent. She herself did not believe in violence but if her boys turned slightly boisterous, she let them have their fun; there were some broken bones but all is fair in love and politics!

The D-day came, she toured the various booths with her men, all was going smoothly, as planned, all were voting for her, the supporters reassured time and again-well, there were a couple of dissenters but luckily their number was few. There was a small celebration in her office while reports came from far flung booths; yes, Rani Sahiba was the choice of the people!

She sank back in her chair and looked at the motley crowd with amusement tinged with irritation. They were all out to please her, none of them had the courage to ever speak the truth before her, some tried to cloak it to prevent hurting her feelings, some to keep on being paid- but she herself knew, things were not all that bright.

The days passed swiftly before the day of counting. She left Himmatnagar and went to a metropolis to stay in oblivion for a couple of days- away from the intrigues, hassles, gossips, back-biting. Cities have much to offer in the way of anonymity- there was no one who would recognize her in the streets, she could buy whatever she liked wherever she liked, there was no one to comment on her apparel, behavior- this was life! But soon she started missing the love only a small town person knows and a person of her level is used to receiving. She missed being greeted by all and sundry and just before the counting began she returned.

Her housekeeper came to her, "Rani Sahiba, we have only six bottles of champagne, we'll need more after midnight."

"Let me win first, we can always send somebody to buy champagne."

"But you are winning and see the tribals have already started beating their drums and blowing their pipes, they'll have to be fed and they'll want daru"

"Don't do anything till the final results are declared." She retorted a trifle sharply, she was a born pessimist, hence defeats did not break her- she always expected them!

They left her alone- knowing that as the final results were to be declared, she was nervy and jittery. What if she lost? So what, she told herself, she'd have so much time for herself to do whatever she wished. But how could she lose? She was ahead – quite ahead.

She went to the courtyard and sat on the huge marble swing- her mother had designed it and had supervised its making- no wonder it was so beautiful, delicate and sturdy at the same time. Suddenly, she found that she was all alone, even her bassinet hound had left her to sleep in his favorite corner. They would have slept, but was there sleep for her?

But how could they sleep? Sleep was a luxury that people in politics could never indulge in. Far from the forests came the howl of the wolves that prowled at this time. Her beautiful palace was so isolated that the forest took over where the boundary wall ended and often leopards would wander in the palace gardens in search of prey- her precious dogs.

It was early morning! Precisely 4a.m.! And nobody came near to inform her of the results! What carelessness! How could all of them go off to sleep? She bent to retrieve her cigarette packet. It was empty. She patted the pockets in her ghaghra. These days she had taken to wearing ghaghra choli- traditional, comfortable, convenient, one could sleep in it and waking up, could meet people without changing! She had to smoke!

"Veera! Veera! Cigarettes!" she called out. The girl crept in, all the lightness, cheerfulness, energy seemed to have been drained from her. Naturally, keeping awake all the nights did not help. She was so loyal, so trusted one could not do without her. As she came near to give the cigarettes there were traces of tears on her cheeks and her eyes were swollen with crying. Was she mourning the husband who had divorced her?

"What's wrong girl? Why do you cry?"

Instead of answering, Veera fled. Slowly her men started trickling in, one by one, downcast faces, tearful, very very quiet. Why was this scene so reminiscent of the nineteen sixtytwo debacle when she had lost? But she could *not* have lost, it was just not possible. She was ahead, she was winning. She summoned her personal secretary. He came to her, eyes downcast, feet shuffling. "Have I lost?" she demanded. "We have lost." He mumbled.

The words were hard upon her, heavy, like a ton of bricks, hot like molten lava in her ears; she could not comprehend what was being said by the people around her. She felt as if she were speaking words of assurance, consoling the people around her; she watched herself act normal, cool, as if an everyday incident had occurred. She saw that she ordered the housekeeper to serve tea and snacks, none had eaten in the night. She herself took a cup and nearly gagged on it. She saw herself strongly voicing her plans to gather forces and start afresh. "So what if they lost the assembly elections, the Parliament, the Rajya Sabha, they were beckoning." saying so she saw that she had straightened herself and stood up. Taking that as a cue, the men began to leave. She dragged herself to her bedroom and there in its pretty basket her favorite bassinet pup lay dead.

All her reserves broke down and as her senses came back with the shock, she dissolved in tears. This was the ultimate sort of defeat that could be inflicted on her- man and beast, both had deserted her. What worse fortune could befall her?

She cried herself dry and then when she could not weep anymore she took control of herself. Veera came with a large mug of "neera" for her- neera, the juice extracted from the date trees- her favorite early morning drink. Taking the mug, she summoned her dogs- Czar, Czarina, Toffee, Blinkey, Tiger, Purdy, Steffi, Chocolate and so many more. Not knowing of her defeat, they were the same, they leaped around her, licking her face, pawing her and led the way for her customary walk.

She entered her huge gardens- Oh! The red silk cotton was in bloom. How magnificent it looked behind its background of the azure sky! And the orange hibiscus too had a flower- she noted that the grafting she'd done on it had worked. The grass was green all over. The mango trees were laden with blossoms and a truly intoxicating scent pervaded the atmosphere. Why hadn't she noticed it before? Well, where was the time?

"Jai Jai Rani Sahiba" she was interrupted in her reverie. A couple of tribals stood before her. "Settle our problem." She wanted to retort sharply- "Go to him for whom you have voted" but good sense prevailed. They sensed her hesitation. "No matter what happens, you are still our Rani Ma."- they said. Ah! Nectar, sweet nectar after the molten lava.

Combined with the bounties of Nature and the bounties of human love, her heart was replete. She had no time for these small things which gave her the greatest pleasure, she had no time for the dear tribals, she had no time to enjoy all she had- but now tomorrow seemed to beckon her with the freshness and cheerfulness of a dream- this new, unborn tomorrow was hers to revel in and enjoy. No, she was not defeated. She had gained a victory. She had emerged more than victorious. And tomorrow was another day, the future something to be tried for and won again.

SEVEN

It also Rains in Summer

LeavesFalling…
Feeling the dark veins burst as I tread…
-Doris Lessing

But why tread over them when you have such bonds with them, Saira wonders as she reads these lines again and again in a poem about leaves. Then self consciously she looks at the piles of chinar leaves she is kicking and treading as she goes towards college. She removes her hijab, shakes her head and frees her hair from the barette till it spreads all over her and runs, runs fast singing all the while. And it had to happen- she trips and was going to fall heavily when two khaki clad arms support her and make her stand,. Indian soldier! She is terrified and remains rooted to the spot!

But he smiles, a very warm smile and she notes he is just like one of the boys at her college. "Going to the college?" he asks, noting the books in her hand. She nods. "You do speak, don't you?" he asks impishly. She laughs at that and says "yes" and smiles, her dimples more pronounced.

"But I should not be walking with you" she dimples "neither should I" he agrees. "if my brother sees, I will have to face hell." And then both laugh, so loudly that more chinar leaves fall and some birds chirp loudly-scolding them for this noise.

"Where are you from, Indian soldier?"

"I am from Bihar, Kashmiri girl."

"Do you like it here?" she asks.

"If I had a friend, I would have really liked it."

"Now my college is nearing, bye." She says hastily tying her hair and wearing her hijab. Arjun smiles and steps aside. He watches her go.

The same time the next day he manages to get guard duty in that area. She wears a red phiran and long red danglers that toss about as she speaks. They exchange names.

"Why in a hurry, Kasmiri mirch?" he asks.

"Because I have college, Bihari Babu!" she replies merrily.

"How did you know of such a name?"

"Have I not heard of Shatrughan Sinha?" "Oh you have, have you?" "Yes, Mr. Litti- Chokha!"

How he laughed when she said so, amazed that she knew such things!

"Okay, Miss Roganjosh, can you cook?" She dimples at him and says "yes".

"But I want proof."

"Why should I supply proof?"

And pouting she runs off.

The next day he is late. The Commanding Officer had summoned him with other men and orders were being issued regarding further security measures. He surreptitiously looked at his watch. The time was fast approaching and he had not even started! As soon as he could leave decently, he left- walking briskly and then breaking into a fast sprint. Yes! She was there! Alone, admiring the trees; pulling her green shawl closer around her.

"You are late today."

"Duty calls"

"What duty?"

"We were getting some work orders."

"See what I have brought you."

She gives a small packet, still warm. He unwraps it-four kebabs lie there. His heart sings.

"Did you make them?"

"No, the girl around the corner! You fool! I made them for you! You wanted proof of my cooking, so there!"

"Sit by my side while I taste them."

She sat demurely pulling her phiran over her knees.

He bit into the kebab. It was delicious. "You have a bite" She refuses. They hear the tinkle of goat bells. She runs off. He stands straight, changing his demeanor to strict and alert.

For two days it rained very heavily. He knew she would not come, yet he would stand in his mackintosh. The third day the sun broke through the clouds, the birds chirped merrily again, squirrels ran races on tree trunks and Saira came skipping.

"What do you study?" he asks. "Are you a professor or my father?" she demands. "You first want proof and then you ask what I do in college. I don't kill flies. I study." She stamps her foot. He picks up that foot and puts it between his palms. It was dainty, pink, covered with toe rings, red nail polish and such pretty cloth shoes.

"Now if you leave my foot I can go to college." She says.

"Suppose I don't"

"I will complain to your C.O"

"Go, complain, he will say women must listen to their men folk.'

She wrenches her foot away and sprints down laughing all the while.

There is a letter from home. Mother is ill and keeps on taking his name. He is the only child. He is not married and that is her sorrow- had he married there would have been a daughter-in-law to look after her, grandchildren tumbling in the courtyard. Father is also not well. Every day they wait for some news of his, that maybe he would return soon. They are also very afraid that he is in Kashmir for soldiers get killed so easily there. He becomes homesick and as he sits under the chinar trees, remembering the mango trees of his village, the huge rice fields that could be seen from one end of the horizon to the other, his mother puffing rotis hot, covered with ghee she had made with thick arahar dal and alu gobi ki sabzi. He can feel the taste on his tongue. He can hear his mother's sweet imploring, "Take one more, Babua." Tears fill his eyes.

"Why does my Fauji cry?" Her palms brush away the tears. Did she say "my" fauji? A smile rose to his lips. She sits close to him. He puts his arm around her, her head on his shoulder. Is this bliss he asks himself. He hears boots, both leap aside and in a twinkling she is gone.

There is a commotion in Saira's home. Her grandmother is angry. She is angry that everyday some food is missing. A couple of days back, four kebabs were gone, after that two parathas, then roasted corn on the cob and she could swear someone had even raided the Yakhni pot. Today she has made rogan josh and already she sees a good one fourth missing. It has to be the new maid who steals this food and she must be dealt with.

Saira trembles at this injustice. How can she confess to her grandmother for whom she takes all that food? Now she wonders, if her family would get to know about the fauji what would happen! Anyway she must tell her grandmother that she was taking the food everyday for a hungry friend. Why hungry? Has illness at home? It sounded easy but when repeated to her grandmother it was tough. The old lady's eyes bore into her.

"Who is this friend, granddaughter? Bring her home, we must see her." She blushes. Mother and grandmother are quick to notice it and exchange glances.

"Take your brother along when you go to college, you run off like the spring wind." Mother admonishes.

He is surprised to see her with a ten year old boy. She motions with her forefinger- Don't talk, he moves back into the trees. The boy leaves her near the college gate and runs back,. She runs to the chinar trees. "What happened?" he asks, scared for her. "Mother and grandmother are suspicious."

"Why? Who saw us?"

"Nobody but food was missing; they were blaming the maid so I confessed."

"What! You told them about me?" he is aghast.

"Fool! I said it's for a hungry girl!"

Both laugh until they hear the college girls passing.

The letter from home is heavier this time. He slits the envelope with a piece of chinar twig. A photograph falls. He looks at two dreamy eyes and a smiling face. She is Nutan whom he has to marry when he goes home next month. His parents feel that she will be the ideal daughter-in-law. He closes his eyes and Saira comes before him, laughing like the brook that ripples down the valley.

Can he imagine Saira in his courtyard? Can he imagine her pressing his mother's feet? Can he imagine her bringing food for his father, head covered demurely?

Could he ever imagine that the elders of the village would accept a Muslim girl and let her live there?

And what about Saira's family? If they came to know about him what measures would they take to prevent and punish? With a heavy heart he put the letter and photograph aside and made his decision.

Next day the girl waited under the chinars, moving from one tree to another till it became very late. Unhappily she threw a packet near the spring and walked away. Soon a squirrel, two sparrows and a crow uncovered the four, warm kebabs.

EIGHT

Mandla

Long, long before the Khadi brigade chose to dissect this wonderful noble state, The Central Provinces, as called by the British which again became Madhya Pradesh; long before man's greed became more and more visible defying the times when man and beast had learnt to live together, long before the impact of Industrial Revolution could be felt in this area and quick, devastating changes could be made; Mandla was a place for Royalty. Ruled by noble kings, she had slowly diminished in stature till she was reduced to a mere principality.

Like the various small "royal" clans that dotted Purnea in Bihar, similarly such clans could be found near and about Mandla; impoverished, living in the past, trying to keep up their prestige and somehow eking out a living from the rough terrain. It was especially more difficult for widows. There was so much at stake for them. First there was the "purity" factor when anyone could point a finger at them and say that they had relations with such and such person-anyone could be named. After such ignominy it would be very difficult for that person to retain the honour that goes with royalty and either she would leave the palace with thousands of her kind to join Vrindavan or Varanasi or brazen it out. Few had the thick skin to do so.

Genteel poverty is torturous, especially if once there was a steady flow of money and luxury was taken for granted. . These small royal houses, "kingdoms" they would call themselves, had to keep up with the earlier pomp and grandeur somehow and many a time some bracelets or heavy necklaces were slipped to a fiercely loyal servant to be sold to complete the needful- the needful could be ranging from fixing a leaking roof to feeding a hundred sadhus. Somehow they existed; honored and revered by the local people, icons of the golden age of royalty and grandeur. Many had turned to small businesses like hotels and schools. Nearly all depended on agriculture, leaning heavily on wild life that provided game for the table and entertainment for guests.

Near the banks of the Narmada there was such a small state- the state of Roopnagar. The ruler had long succumbed to Bachhus and left an embittered widow, mountains of debts and a very beautiful nineteen year old daughter. The scions of the neighbor "states" had sent messages to find out more about her but once they got to know of the penury and the debts linked with her, the mere topic was dropped and the girl vowed not to marry anyone from royalty or such lineage.

Vidya Devi was a determined little miss, right from the beginning, with a mind of her own. From birth she had seen the struggle her poor mother was subjected to, the degenerate ways of her father- consuming alcohol and nothing else right from the morning till he dropped off- the visits of known courtesans-first they were cultured beauties who knew how to behave, how to speak, so that even girls from noble families could learn from them-somewhat the geisha girls of Japan. Till they came, presented their dadras and thumris and took whatever was given to them with good grace (aapka diya hi to khaate hain) she enjoyed it all, watching them behind the chik curtains. When money became very low and entertainment was mandatory, the cheap brothel types were called. Then her mother told her not to sit behind the chik and after their cheap numbers were over, would throw the notes on the floor. Even then they would pick it up and bow with good grace. Such were the times. But her father was denied nothing. When he demanded anything, her mother merely pursed her lips, saw that the order was followed and looked even more bitter. Before all the money could totally be wiped out, he died.

Vidya being the only child was the sole heir. Mother and daughter tried to plan in the best possible way to survive and survive with dignity. The old palace was crumbling, infested with all kinds of animals, leaking badly and various portions could not be considered safe at all. Some gent had come to them and suggested that they sell the palace to a businessman who would renovate it and start a hotel. He had quoted a good price. The whole night the mother and daughter duo thrashed out the matter, its pros and cons, what would be good for their dignity but bad for their future and then came to the decision that it was better to sell off and live on the interest it would provide. They would shift to the small outhouse which had four rooms, was much more comfortable and manageable. But, what about their dignity? Their position? Both can be damned they agreed and laughed with relief.

It was a comedown, or real comedown the locals said, so used to the watchman, old and doddering who sat at the "Singh Dwar," the massive door which allowed them entry inside, a reminder of past glory. But now? It was like any other home- the bell or knocker would be sounded, anyone could enter anytime.

Now the servants- most had land in their names so they could go back to tilling it- she had nothing to pay them, the Rajmata told them frankly. Nearly all, wiping their rheumy eyes filled with tears, said they only wanted to serve her. But, she reasoned, it was important that they live with their families now and visit her from time to time. They left. The household expenses now came down to one fourth of what she was spending earlier. There was money in the bank after a long long time. There was no perpetually drunk tyrant stating his filthy desires and there was no reason to pawn off the remainder of jewelry to some cheap female who for an hour of prancing around would walk off with something precious- whatever he had considered necessary to give. There was peace.

Peace there was but along with it a lot of emptiness, no sense of direction. There was no reason to welcome the morning Vidya would say, I need to do something. Vidya was an M.A and had no formal training in Education but she thought she would manage and started a small nursery school along with two other girls who were her age and were Montessori trained. The school was started in the stables.

The last mare had been sold off decades ago and the entire building lay in utter neglect and ruin. It had taken a full week to have the place thoroughly cleaned out and the garbage burnt. As old saddles and reins and such equestrian paraphernalia were being added to the slowly growing pile to be burnt, her heart became heavy. She had come from such stock- her grandfather was renowned for his skill in horsemanship and was the best polo player around. Why had her father degenerated so?

Anyway, the long building of the stables now stood with only sturdy walls and a tile roof. After white washing and painting it soon began to have the look she wanted. She chose a bright red and sunny yellow and orange and lime green and after all the fairies and animals and cartoon characters had been painted, pretty moulded plastic furniture arranged, toys brought, she was at last ready to start.

They called the school "Kislaya", the tiny red leaves that first appear on a plant. The town was abuzz with all these developments and many eager parents lined up with their toddlers for admission! Vidya was delighted! It was a new role she was playing now. The dainty girl who was hardly seen in public, what to say of communicating with all and sundry, now found herself to be the centre of attraction of people, some who came merely to gape open-mouthed. The way the mother and daughter had managed to change their lives was in general commended highly by nearly all, especially the younger generation who felt how right it was to ring out the old and ring in the new. From being objects of pity they became an inspiration to such fate-stricken people who saw what could be done to their lives if they only had the courage to start afresh.

In mid-session, if there is a midsession in a nursery school, a very handsome young man came with two small, chubby boys in tow. She found out that he worked in the Railways and had just been transferred to Mandla. He had recently lost his wife. The boys needed special care so he had brought them to her school. Was there any provision for the boys to stay after school till five in the evening, there was no one at home and the boys were so small and missed their mother so much? His eyes filled as he spoke and unwarily she agreed, knowing that the two maids they had retained could look after the boys well. Anyway, whose heart would not melt to see those tiny woebegone faces, poor motherless souls, she would surely help them.

So began a friendship which was fulfilling for both sides. Vidya at last got company. The Rajmata and she would wait for five- fifteen when he would enter their gate. Despite his protesting vehemently each time, they insisted that he have tea and some snacks with them along with the children. He in turn would bring news of the outer world to them- news that no one would tell them of- no one was so free with them and neither were they so free so as to ask. So any new object that was being sold in the market, any gossip, any national/international news, he was the provider and how they enjoyed every bit of it! Also, he was an excellent singer. When this talent of his was revealed suddenly one rainy day when he hummed some lines and Vidya clamored for more, it became a regular feature that some singing had to take place in the evening after tea accompanied by the sitar played by Vidya.

The little boys drew closer to Vidya and found all their happiness in that four roomed house. When this friendship blossomed into romance it's difficult to say but one day it did. The Rajmata was averse to it but in the racing tide she too was swept away and before she could realize what was happening she had given her permission for marriage as luckily they were of the same caste.

"We don't know anything about him," she stated her fears.

"But we do, he is a railway employee, having a little land."

"But his ancestry? His lineage?"

"If he questions me about mine, will I not die a dozen deaths when I tell him about my father and his debts and..."

"That will be enough." This silenced whatever talk both were coming with.

He was adamant about one matter- she was to go and stay with him_ he would not live in her house. The mother-daughter argued, pleaded, coaxed, cajoled but no, he was firm. So Vidya agreed.

The marriage itself was a very simple and sober affair. She asked him about his family, his brothers and sisters and anyone else he would have liked to invite. He said "Nobody".

"But why?"

"When my wife died, no one came, no one even bothered to find out what happened to my boys. Now they are not my family. My only family is you and the boys.". She understood. She too had faced so many slights, so many put downs that she understood.

"You will always be a step-mother, Vidya" the mother reminded.

"No my two boys will love me."

"Imagine having two boys even before marriage- What a strain! What a huge responsibility!"

"I can manage" she had stated confidently.

So amidst all misgivings, worries and fears, romance won and they were married.

She came to his house. He had bought it after selling whatever he had in his own village, his native Madhubani. The house was old, dark inside, rather untidy. The main three rooms had asbestos roofing, the verandah that jutted out had thatch. There was a courtyard, a tap where a brave guava tree struggled. She stood, surveying everything, resolving to make pleasant changes, make it home.

The two little boys clutched at the ends of her heavy bridal saree, all awonder to see her dressed so, with so many pieces of jewelry too. She went to the space he used as a kitchen. There were hardly a few utensils and some containers, a coal choolah and some blackened pots, the stone grinder and pestle-that was all. All right she had enough to make it going, no problem. She was surprised that he was nowhere around. She stood in the courtyard looking at the deepening darkness one boy holding her hand the other her pallu.

Suddenly he appeared. There were two boys with him- one would be about ten, the other twelve- both looked so much like him, his carbon copies! Were they his brothers?

"Vidya, I have a confession to make. I have two more sons. This is Jayesh and this Roopesh. They stay in a hostel in the town from the time their mother died. They have come to see you."

Mother of four sons! What could she say to this! Her head reeled and she sat heavily on the courtyard floor- there was nothing to sit upon.

"Why didn't you tell me earlier?"

"You would have never accepted me."

"But was it fair to conceal the truth?"

"No it wasn't but I could not lose you-"

She saw the solemn expression on the faces of the elder boys and felt ashamed. She smiled at them. Their faces lit up and they came closer.

"Now that you have come, we may stay in our home, New Mother". Roopesh the younger said, a little afraid.

"Shhh! Keep quiet!" admonished the older one, "She can't look after so many of us". Evidently he must have been coached by his father earlier.

Her sweet nature surfaced and she smiled. "Of course you will stay here, no one will let you stay in a hostel now. But first of all let's see what is there to eat." She noted that at the mention of food how happy they looked.

Food there was a-plenty. Her mother had seen to it; there were big boxes and earthen pots full of dry sweets and syrupy ones. There were earthen pots of freshly set creamy curd, sacks of flat rice, huge moulds of jaggery. One of the various boxes that had come as her trousseau held kitchen items so she set about finding it.

The new steel plates shone in the darkness as she seated the father and his four sons on new sheets in the courtyard and served them pressed rice, curd and sweets. How all of them ate! Her heart went out to the motherless ones. No, she had not been shortchanged. She had got a bonus!

NINE

One Winter Morning

Maya wrapped the shawl closely about her but her shivering did not stop. “It must be freezing outside,” she thought but even inside the train it was no better. Though she was so warmly dressed, the chattering of her teeth would not stop. No wonder that the compartment was nearly empty. Rather scary at five o’clock on a winter morning to be sitting alone in a train with your nearest fellow traveler seven berths away but she had no option. The telegram came late at night that her mother was seriously ill and this was the earliest train. Thank God it took only five hours and she would soon be with her mother. And it all had to take place when Ramesh was on tour! She left a note and the keys of the house with her neighbor-nearly missed the train due to that gossiping woman, but one had to bear with her as she was so helpful.

The train chugged on and Maya put her feet up and wrapped her arms around her knees to get warmer,. She ought to have got a blanket along but it did not strike her then- life was still passing in a haze, a blur. She had been married for six months only and life was so sweet. Could any man be better than her Ramesh? How lucky she had been to have him. Suppose she had not listened to her mother and fallen in the "trap" (as her mother was so fond of saying) of that long- haired freak who had appeared to her the most romantic person on earth, what would have been her fate now? Later she heard that he became an alcoholic and took drugs. He worked with her in her section of the insurance company and was such an ardent fan and devoted follower that one had to be sweet on him.

She was interrupted in her reverie when her train jolted to a halt. She peered through the window and saw that it was Itawah. A lot of people were waiting on the station. She was glad- it was getting too lonely all by herself. There was a commotion and suddenly her compartment was full. How could so many people venture at this time she wondered, she had a genuine cause but they? May be they had it too. The last to enter when the train had nearly started were two men, both chewing pan and with them was a burqa clad lady. Maya turned her face away and hoped that they would not sit on her berth – then all the time they'd bend past her as she was sitting near the window, to put their mouth out to spit. Disgusting! But her berth had only a hefty Punjabi lady who had already taken out her beads and was murmuring her prayers and just next to her was another lady who could have fitted in any part of the country as she looked quite nondescript. She too had wrapped her shawl around herself tightly and had even covered her head with it. The burqa clad lady came between them- came? Rather, she hopped, skipped and jumped between them, aided by one of the two who were accompanying her and sat between her and the nondescript sort. Goodness knows why she walked that way and needed so much aid to walk a few steps- maybe she had an operation or had some sort of defect or whatever. Why should one bother and Maya turned back to her window to look at the sunrise.

"Ek minute," it was one of those fellows, had a furry cap on, and just in time Maya removed her head for he pushed his head near the window and squirted a large red stream of betel-juice outside. Maya looked at him with revulsion. Filthy beast. Fur Cap was sitting on the berth just across hers with his mate Black Jacket. Surprisingly, they did not talk at all and just kept staring at either her or the fan. She was used to being stared at, being the beauty she was but it irked her very much now and she glared at them. Then she found out that they were not staring at her but at the burqa- clad lady next to her who came with them. Funny! She thought they could have done all the staring at home moreover what can one see on a burqa that one can stare so long! The tea-vendor came and everyone had tea. Maya cupped her hands around the glass to warm them and even held her glass at the tip of her nose to warm them- it was freezing so badly. It was thick, hot and syrupy sweet but in the cold it was very welcome. As she handed the glass back to the vendor she saw that Burqa wasn't having tea. Instinctively she looked across- Fur Cap and Black Jacket were having theirs in big gulps. Selfish brutes- most probably poor Burqa did not have any money on her – the old fashioned ones never carried any and so these brutes bought tea only for themselves without giving her any. Some men were like that. They'd themselves eat, drink and be merry but forget their wives totally. Ramesh was so wonderful that all such men should be inspired by him to change. Now which one of them could be her husband? Which one looked the worst?

She decided that Fur Cap had the more villainous look and then Black Jacket- her brother? How foolish! No brother worth his rakhi would have tea himself and not ask his sister. Step- brother? No, they too had to keep up appearances. Ah! He must be the husband's brother. Yes, that fitted.

The Sardarni had long finished her prayers and had her tea- so she turned to the nondescript woman and asked the inevitable question- where was she going? It seemed that the two had the same destination and soon they were chatting like old friends- nondescript was a nursery school teacher, Sheela, while she started addressing the Sardarni "Behenji". After they had finished getting informed about each other's husbands, their jobs, their children (number and kind with ages) they turned to Burqa "So behen, where are you going?" asked Behenji. Burqa did not reply- there was no movement from her that she had even heard. So behenji did not give up and asked louder. Still no reply but Fur cap and Black Jacket showed annoyance on their faces. Then Sheela spoke up- "Maybe she just wanted to be left alone." Behenji started a long speech-"Its always nice to be sociable- we are all co-passengers, when shall we ever meet again, by talking to each other we merely share our sorrows and joys, life is a journey, isn't it sister?" and she turned to Maya. Maya nodded hastily and started fumbling in her bag to avoid any further questioning. Then all was still.

A blind man came singing a very well –known bhajan very tunefully. Every one gave him money except Burqa and her two companions. "Hard hearted, oh sister, some people are very hard-hearted. Little do they realize that heaven and hell are all on earth and may be if we are good to others we will not have to suffer but if we are not…" and she checked her tongue and looked pointedly at Burqa. No response whatsoever; just another round of glaring from Fur Cap and Black Jacket. Luckily the next station came so any altercation which could have taken place was prevented.

Just as the train steamed in to the station, most of the passengers, at least the men folk started getting down- some to wander on the platform and stretch their legs and some to buy the samosas that the station was noted for. Had Ramesh been with her she could have had those delicious samosas. There was no question of her getting down, she was just, plain nervous about missing the train- Maya thought ruefully. Then she saw them getting up- should she, shouldn't she? Well, Fur cap and Black Jacket were just not the amiable sort whom you can ask for such things and so she did not say anything and got down. Behenji was the first to have got down- with her bulk people naturally made way otherwise she had no qualm in pushing and pummeling- and was soon back with a handful of samosas- tiny ones sitting on their bed of newspaper.

She offered them to Maya who shyly took them, Sheela too took hers and very graciously Behenji extended them towards Burqa. No response. "All right –people will not say I did not do my duty." Behenji said and started munching her samosas.

Suddenly Burqa lifted her feet and brought them hard on Maya's. Maya shrieked with pain and started rubbing them wondering what had got into her neighbor when she did it again. That was too much. Before Maya could take up cudgels, Behenji rose, arms akimbo and spoke with righteous indignation-"We have borne your insults and bad behavior without a murmur but physical assault is too much." And before she could say anything more, Burqa started beating her feet on the ground. The three women were thunder struck. What had happened to her?

Behenji's good nature came to the fore- "maybe she is uncomfortable and cannot speak. Her men folk are not here too- let's see" and saying that she lifted the burqa and gave a piercing yell. The face beneath the Burqa had a wide piece of sticking plaster taped on her lips! "Oh, you poor girl! Who did this to you!' Saying this Behenji held her face while Sheela and Maya tore off the sticking plaster. Sheela was very thoughtful and quickly took out cold cream from her bag and applied it on the raw marks left by the plaster on the girl's face.

The girl, no lady, (she was in her mid-twenties so what would you call her) was truly a breathtakingly beautiful one. Tears ran down her eyes as she told them to lift her burqa from behind. They did so and to their horror they saw that her hands and feet were tied behind too – so she had walked like that, thought Maya.

They quickly untied her and meanwhile the compartment was filling fast. Behenji was shouting to all and sundry about the happenings and she waited near the door to personally "see" Black Jacket and Fur Cap – not the husband and his younger brother but *Kidnappers*. But they would have heard the commotion and were nowhere to be seen when the Railway Police carried out a search.

After the lady was freed and her wrists and ankles were massaged vigorously, she nearly fell unconscious. The entire compartment and many others besides rushed to get water and tea. You see the word had spread that the look alike of Madhuri Dixit was there, so many came to gape and gawk and some felt that the services rendered then would be helpful later in striking up a long and lasting friendship. Soon she became normal enough to tell her story.

She was Naseem Rehman, a lecturer who had just taken up a job at Delhi in a Women's College. She was new to the place and often lost her way and that particular day when she was kidnapped, she saw that Fur Cap and Black Jacket were following her. She remembered seeing them every day near the college gate and became very afraid. She'd just broken into a run when a white Maruti van drove very near, and the engine still running, the doors were slid open. Fur Cap and Black Jacket pushed her inside climbed after her and the first thing they did was to tape her mouth. Then they told her that if she behaved, she would come to no harm otherwise they would have no compunctions in having fun with her and then putting a bullet through her head.

They tied her hands and ankles and put a burqa over her to conceal it. Their plan was to take her to an Arab who dealt in such matters and sell her. Then the Arab could either take her to his country or re-sell her, it would be as he pleased.

She burst into tears now and scores of handkerchiefs were offered. You must note, that now the more sympathetic were the young men who rushed to her whenever they felt she needed something. Now everybody could not stand near the berth and hear a first person account of the happening so many gathered around the windows and those too unfortunate to find a place in near proximity demanded to know what was happening and a running commentary, well spiced with the commentator's own imagination and vocabulary was passed on.

The girl resumed her story. It seemed that they had a quarrel over the previous debts with the driver of the car, so he coolly dumped them and drove off. They did not dare to hire another car lest the driver be suspicious and either report them to the police or demand a share so they thought the train would be the next best thing. As she was tied and gagged so there was no danger of her asking for help and nobody in their farthest of dreams would think that such a daring act would be committed in a crowded train!

"And you know the rest." She whispered and then folded her hands- "I will forever be grateful to these ladies who have saved me."

The three concerned looked, according to their natures, smug; pleased and embarrassed. The Railway Police came to have an account of what had happened and took her away but before that Behenji rose and drew herself to her full height (an imposing figure she made) and said very loudly- "Daughter, please give me your address and telephone number so that I can confirm from your home whether you have reached safely. These days one cannot trust anybody and many times those who are supposed to protect do the most harm." And much to the anger-tinged embarrassment of the police, she took down their names also. "Who knows" she said, "Seeing such a beautiful girl, one's ideas might change. Even a Vishwamitra broke his vows when he saw Menaka."

A titter arose in the compartment and Naseem got down. The entire compartment waved their hankies or neckties from the windows long after she could not be seen.

ONE MONTH LATER

Maya was at home making tea when the door bell rang, "Ramesh, please answer it." Ramesh opened the door, there was some small talk, the door closed and Ramesh gave a loud whistle.

"Maya! Who are the Rehmans? Look what they have sent!"

Maya rushed out and saw a huge gift hamper and a bouquet of two dozen roses with a card- "Thank you for helping our daughter."

"Which daughter? whom did you help?"

"What had happened?" Ramesh was all eagerness.

In her mother's illness the girl had been so busy and later in her household affairs that she had completely forgotten the matter.

"You see, it all happened one winter morning," she began.

TEN

The General's Wife

She looked at her watch and increased her speed. There was no point at all in being so late that the pitch dark grounds would be deserted and she would be the solitary walker. She had to be careful of the jagged stones that dotted that part of the road, and nearly tripping, she reached the stairs. Gone were the days when she could take them two at a time, and even at that pace she would become breathless by the time she reached the top stair. As usual she paused there to get her breath back and to gaze and gaze at the simple but beautiful garden the retired general's wife had made around the cottage. It had such freshness to it that she would choose spots to admire everyday- some day it would be the pink geraniums, all in one size, all blooming profusely, another day the bell shaped, white dhatura flowers, sweetly intoxicating.

Today just as she focused on the lilies, there stood the general's wife, with a big smile, red sweater and blue jeans, her white shock of hair framing her elfin face.

"Hi, going for a walk?"

"Hi, yes."

"But you are so punctual! I can set the clock by you!"

"But you are the slim one!" Dr. Bhatt complimented. Yes she was slim. She must have been on the wrong side of sixty but she looked so fresh, so youthful!

"But you are the beauty!" she complimented back and both burst into peals of laughter. It was nice to praise and be praised- it sent a warm feeling inside a person.

"Won't you ever stop for a cup of tea, Dr. Bhatt? I have stopped asking dreading another refusal."

Dr. Bhatt laughed apologetically- "One day I'll invite myself over and then we'll swap stories and howlers about our teaching days," she knew that the general's wife had been a teacher. Immediately she brightened. "Oh you must! And when are you inviting me to judge a competition? Last time you promised but you did not."

She contemplated for a moment then remembered the recitation competition to be held in her school next month and promptly invited her.

"Of course I'll come, is it all right if I come in jeans?"

"You can come in anything provided you are covered and had the audience been women only, I would not even have said that!"

Uproarious, gut-wrenching laughter followed, much to the confusion of the passers-by, a young man with a dog and two college girls who wondered what the two elderly ladies had to laugh about, as if the domain of laughter belonged solely to the young!

Dr. Bhatt rushed and completed her customary three rounds of the playground that would complete a kilometer, and rushed home. She was always rushing-rushing home, rushing to school, rushing to classes, to market, the list was endless. Not that rushing saved her time, it was just the way she was, why walk when you can run?

The next day in school after the second period, she saw some pink geraniums and remembered the general's wife. She took out her black diary to write her name in the list of judges when suddenly… suddenly, the chirping of the birds on the apricot tree seemed fainter, the forests that were far seemed to move away farther still, and she held the table for support.

As her head cleared one thought pounded in her brain… the general's wife had died in an accident exactly a year back.

ELEVEN

The Pensive Mason

Dr. Bhatt clucked her tongue in exasperation! The slip-shod work would not do at all! She called out to the mason- “Nageenaji, what is this? Is such work expected out of a seasoned mason like you?” the man shuffled his feet, rubbed his cement encrusted hands on his blood red shirt, gave a polite cough and began his long list of excuses. She listened to all of them as patiently as she could manage, her foot tapped with impatience at times when thinking of the pending work on her table; ultimately the scholar in her won, for instead of giving him a sharp rejoinder, she marveled at his choice of words as well as his polite way of speaking! Amazing! He should have been in the teaching profession!

Lunch time came. She felt sorry for the mason and his helper who would go to their room and eat whatever was there while she had so much! With her typical energetic zeal she set the cooker and soon fragrant rice was made, dal and vegetables were already there. She called them for lunch and was delighted to see their surprised, expectant faces. ““Why did you bother, you have so much work yourself?” mumbled the mason and she noted again his choice of words, he must be well educated! Then why this work? This thought nagged her until she tapped her head to get rid of it, as she heaped the food on their plates. She put some ghee, some pickles (who would give them these), and wondered about their lives. A little later she was content to see that they had polished their plates.

The mason's helper had the name of a prince- Chandrabhan- and the demeanor of a camel- slow, unhurried keeping to his own pace, regardless of what was being told or expected. She was very carefully polite in addressing such people- "Chandrabhanji, will you please come here, then we can plan what to do with the remainder marble chips." He ambled graciously, delighted by the "we", forming a sort of camaraderie with the educated lady and himself. Squatting on his haunches, he looked at the various sacks piled there, rattling off what they contained. Suddenly mid-way he stopped and said, "I must go, have to give medicine to masonji." Dr. Bhatt looked at his retreating figure and laughed to herself, what a hurry he was in, all of a sudden! At least he could move fast!"

As Chandrabhan joined her in heaping the chips, she asked casually, "What medicine did you give him?"

"Tablet".

"That's fine, but what was it for?"

The man shuffled uneasily, blew at his hands, wrapped the checked towel tightly round his head and looked rather uncomfortable.

"Masonji is a very good man."

"I know that but I wanted to know why you had to give him medicine."

"You are a kind lady, so I will tell you," he lowered his voice confidentially, "our masonji was a college student, then during anti-reservation riots something happened and he had to be put in the mental asylum and then in jail. So now he has to do this work for a living."

"But what had he done?" Dr. Bhatt was puzzled.

"He had strangled many elderly women. And if he is not given medicine on time, this problem recurs."

Dr. Bhatt had to sit down.

TWELVE

Birds Of A Feather

In the early fifties going to attend the highly auspicious Kumbh snan was a very risky as well as arduous job. First of all there was the crowd- a stupendous, milling thousands who seemed to merge into one, forming a behemoth that would lose direction and move from one place to another, the horrified, scared individual being carried forth by them. The women were usually veiled- that led to more problem and they would follow the feet going in front of them and may be a familiar garment and if luck was averse, some other person would be wearing the same garment and all sorts of problems would arise from that!

The means of communication was rudimentary- all depending on the loud speaker that would bellow names from time to time of lost people. Even those announcers had much to face for the dutiful wives would not take the names of their husbands and the announcers had to make wild guesses on the basis of hints provided- a lady would point to a green chilli- O, Hari then the picture of Ram and then the Ramayana, so they would put together that the husband was Hari Ram! But undaunted by such hurdles, the announcers would call out names, trying to put families together, lost children, wives, mothers.

Such a crying, disheveled and a very upset family came to them. It was a large family with a retinue of servants, old but yet sturdy grandparents, the veiled daughter-in-law sobbing uncontrollably, the son looking very nervous and wishing to pacify his wife but not daring to so under the glare of the maternal eye. The crying of a baby made the announcers realize that beneath the veil and tears was also a baby.

The grandfather cleared his throat, banged his stick on the ground for effect and said "Our baby is missing." Upon querying it was found that she was the twin of the six month baby crying in her mother's lap. One by one everyone had bathed in the Ganga, even the babies had their dip. The lost baby was dressed and handed over to the maid servant. The baby had solid gold bracelets, chain and tiny tops in its ears. She was a very cherubic, sunny baby. A lady had come to the maid servant and after much wheedling had taken the baby from her and was playing with it. A bangle -seller was passing and the maid servant had just turned her face for a second when the lady and the baby were gone.

Another veiled sobbing woman must be the errant maid! No, she could not be in cahoots with anyone for her family had worked in their family for more than four generations so it was not possible. It was only carelessness that led to such a loss. And girls were treasured in their family, the old gentleman hastened to say.

Call after call was made, the announcers, relentless in their search called out till the last day even after the family had departed leaving its address. But nothing could be known and the whereabouts of the baby was swallowed in the waves of the Ganga.

Years passed.

....

Reshma Bai was sunning herself on her balcony, her long silky hair loose. This evening she was leaving for Surat. A very rich family had invited her to do a mujra on their daughter's wedding. How far Surat seemed to the Lucknavi girl! She was not yet nineteen and considered to be the prize courtesan of the entire area. It was not merely her beauty everyone swore, there were other pink- cheeked, voluptuous girls to choose from, but she was a class apart. There was a dignity about her which was rarely seen in the modern courtesans, a dignity with such poise, such serenity and composure that the viewer was bound to feel that something akin to devotion should be bestowed on her. To enhance such an image, she was very choosy about where she went to or who she would permit to visit her. Her initial schooling was done in a convent far away, long before she got to know who she was and what was expected out of her so her English was impeccable. It was a unique combination- excellent Urdu with impeccable British- English- no wonder, the clients were floored immediately!

But how bewildered, how heartbroken she was when she got to know that her destiny was not different from her mother's! Like the girls of her class, she had dreamed of a good career for herself- may be a doctor, or a lawyer or a teacher- but being a full time courtesan! That was something she did not even dream of! But she had a sneaking fear that one day she would have to take up the family profession- her mother was insistent that she be regular with her Kathak classes and her classical singing. Her mother was a perfectionist and so in no way did she want her daughter to lack in any field.

"But I could have taken up a respectable career!" Reshman had wailed.

"No career is respectable for a woman- everywhere there are pitfalls and she has to comply with the wishes of her superiors for peanuts! It is in this profession that you can have the best company around you who will provide much for the quality time you give them!"

"But I will be no better than a prostitute!"

"No! A courtesan is different! She is very cultured, educated and is so well- versed in all matters pertaining to art, culture and etiquette that a few decades ago, girls from the royal family were sent to them to learn "tehzeeb"- etiquette."

So Reshma wiped her tears.

Her first "mujra" was a disaster. She found that despite her rigorous training, her foot work went wrong, her ghungroos felt leaden on her ankles, she could not bear the leers of the gathered "august" personage and she hated every minute of it! How wonderful it was to go to her room and remove all the paraphernalia needed for the evening, unclip and loosen all the heavy, flashy jewelry on her, wipe out all the makeup and sit in bed in her nightie sipping hot milk.

"Amma, I don't want to do it again."

"Yes, you will."

"But if I study, I can make much more."

"Enough! No more is to be said," her mother thundered and left the room. How Reshma had wept that night! The old maid servant Hamida Bi had come to her and bathed her temples and rubbed oil in her hair and feet to soothe her nerves, all the while muttering over the bad luck that women had to face.

"But I hate these beastly mujras and those horrible people who watch me dance!"

"But my little doll, they pay as well and one has to think of your mother's old age too."

"It's not fair Hamida Khala, that my life has to be led as she wants it- I hate this life, this environment, I want to be respected by people"

"Ah, my child you came from a respectable family!" As soon as she had uttered these words, Hamida could have bitten off her tongue. How many times she had been sworn to secrecy about Reshma and how she had vowed that none would ever know! Now she had let the cat out of the bag!

"Khala! What did you say?" The girl rose from the pillow, her tear-stained face all awash with hope- "Did you say that I came from a respectable family? That means that Amma is not my own mother?"

Hamida kept a stony silence. Knowing Nusrat Jahan's vile temper, she feared the worst- she had her own goons who would kill for a small sum, so she kept quiet. But the girl would not be quiet- she had to know the truth.

"Khala tell me, O tell me khala, who was I and from where I came! How did I enter this place khala?" The girl begged and coaxed and cajoled till Hamida gave in and told her.

She told her about the fateful day of the Kumbh Mela when she was hardly six months old, how Nusrat had taken her from the maid-servant's arms and had run away, such a beautiful girl-child would secure her future, would earn her millions and her old age would be provided for.

The girl listened wide-eyed to this tale. "But who am I? How will I ever know?" the girl cried out.

"You came from a very rich and well known family because long after the Kumbh Mela, your photo was seen in many newspapers for many years where they offered a reward for anyone who would bring information about you."

"Do you have the newspaper?"

"Yes I kept it at the bottom of my trunk, who knows when we might need it, all these years it was hidden with me." They ran to the terrace where Reshma spread the yellowed sheet and saw herself as a baby.

REWARD OF ONE LAC- TO ANYONE WHO GIVES INFORMATION ABOUT THIS BABY. CONTACT AT THE FOLLOWING ADDRESS. PHONE NO....

She greedily devoured the information, reading the address again and again till it was imprinted in her brain and the phone number memorized. They must be rich if they were offering so much reward for the baby girl! And the place was Surat! She had to go to Surat, she would go to her home, tell who she was and have her home and family again. She could leave this beastly life and start afresh! And she was not a Muslim- she was a Hindu! The gentleman who had advertised was one and she would be his grandchild. It was possible that he would have died by this time, who knows. And what their condition would be so many years after one could not say! But a home! A normal home with parents and brothers and sisters- it sounded miraculous for her.

Amidst all this excitement of going to Surat was the greater excitement of meeting her real family! She could not sleep at night because of sheer joy! O she had known it in her bones that she was respectable and did not belong to this dirty crowd! Now she could call them dirty, earlier *this* was family and she also felt it to be disloyal for hadn't she been educated in the convent by this foster mother and till the hateful mujras started, life was very happy for her- so why blame them now?

But the injustice of the act hit her again and again. How unfair it was that she was stolen and brought somewhere else and given a different religion, a different life! But she was careful not to breathe a word or show any hostility towards Nusrat Jahan- somehow she had to escape. Surprisingly she felt no sort of grief at the thought of parting- she would miss only her parrot and Hamida Khala and if the family permitted she would take Khala with her.

....

Surat was not a very big place they said but she felt it was a very big city. As the taxi sped through macadamed roads, she tried to read the signs in Gujarati which was nearly like Hindi. Luckily Nusrat Jahan got high fever and could not come along. Hamida was accompanying her and one of her henchmen Atif. Reshma got the goose bumps whenever she saw him, he looked so evil!

Her mujra was the next evening so she had the whole day to herself as well as the next day. The hotel where they were putting up was not one of the best but very comfortable and rather luxurious. She had a long leisurely bath and was told to rest. Atif was in the next room and warned that she must not venture alone anywhere, though he was impeccably polite but the sweet words had a veiled threat.

Poor Hamida was so tired that she could not keep her eyes open and soon fell fast asleep on the carpet. This was the time! She had seen Atif take a whiskey bottle to his room- soon he would be drunk and fast asleep. Then she could go out and find the address. She had to see her home, her family, no matter what!

....

Seth Dhanpat Rai's bungalow was being decorated with fairy lights. Men were rushing here and there with huge baskets of flowers to adorn the arches. The seth sahib himself all of ninety five years was ensconced in a sofa watching over all the preparations. Everything had to be perfect. His eldest grand-daughter was getting married to the son of the biggest industrialist of Gujarat. They were "simple" people they said and wanted nothing but their "simplicity" was seen on the day of engagement that was held in their home. The guest list ran to five thousand with the topmost caterers out-doing each other, the decoration worth crores and they had gifted much jewelry to his grand- daughter. In no way would he let them be one up. He planned carefully with his son and daughter-in-law for his wife had passed away many years ago- she could never get over the loss of the other twin.

Yes, the girl who was getting married had a twin. So many years ago she was stolen in the Kumbh Mela. The family, for years, had tried to find her, posting advertisements in newspapers, using detectives, but all in vain. His wife felt the loss terribly for it was her idea to take the babies for a holy dip in the Ganga. She would sit quietly by herself, telling her beads and crying softly. She lost interest in the home affairs and the daughter-in-law had to get over her own grief and manage the household which, along with servants of four generations, was more than a hundred.

There were many more people to work than were family members along with widowed aunts and great aunts who had no other home, cousins who came for their education and went onto take up jobs, marry, have children, all the while staying in the huge mansion. Everybody was welcome there. Under the all- pervading eyes of the martinet, the old seth, there was discipline, respect and care for elders and no room for petty squabbles. Mridula, the daughter-in-law was wise and was slowly trained to take up the mantle of the mistress of the house. Hence the home of Seth Dhanpat Rai flourished day by day, the family becoming larger and more expensive.

The old man beckoned to a man servant carrying a tray of sherbet. "Give the workmen before you serve anyone else." He told the man. "Jee Sethji" the man said and left to do as he was bid. "Bapuji, the jewelers have brought the set you wanted Revati to wear, can they come and show you?" This was his only son Gajanan, whose daughter was getting married. The boy was a perfect gem felt the old man – his past virtues were rewarded by God and he was given this son, a true son in all respects, kind, considerate, respectful, humble, always taking his permission, his opinion before doing anything- not that he lacked confidence or caliber, it was merely showing his respect for his father. Ah! He was still handsome, people could mistake him for the groom himself! And the old man gave a low chuckle and said- "Tell them to wait in the Sadar Ghar (drawing room) I am coming."

He had ordered a Navratan set for his beloved Revati. He had seen such jewelry on a Parsi lady decades ago in some party for the elite and had not forgotten it, his sharp, analytical brain had the design etched in it as he had admired it so much and could reproduce it for Shiboo Bhai the topmost jeweler of Surat. Well, let's see what they had done.

Just as he was about to rise, a servant came. "Sethji there is a girl at the gate and she wants to see you."

"Me? There must be some mistake. She must be Revati's friend. Take her inside to Elder sister."

"No, Sethji she insists that she must meet you, she took your name."

"Has she come for a job? Or does she look as if she needed help?"

"She did not say anything, she is very well dressed and seems to come from a good family. She looks quite like our Revati Didi."

"Then I must see her. Send her to me."

....

Reshma had taken a rickshaw after creeping downstairs. She had told the rickshaw puller the address and it was sheer luck that the place was hardly ten minutes from the hotel. As the cold December wind brushed her cheeks, her heart beat wildly. Now it suddenly struck her- would these people accept her, she being what she had become?

They were highly respected in society the gossipmonger rickshaw puller told her and there was a wedding next day itself and after that all the poor of the city would be fed and given new clothes. Only Seth Dhanpat Rai could still do such things. The more Reshma heard of him the more awe struck she became.

The rickshaw stopped at the massive gates of a palatial mansion. The entire length and breadth of the building was being systematically covered with fairy lights. Scores of men were working, putting up arches, decorating with garlands of flowers and leaves, some rushing with trays of hot and cold drinks; amidst all this she felt so small, so low. Anyway, she had nothing to lose and it was her home too.

"I want to speak to the Seth Saheb."

"Elder or younger?" queried the man whom she addressed, he was ticking off something in a notepad.

"Elder" she said.

After a few minutes she was taken inside the gates and to a sofa where a very old man was seated, surrounded by so many men.

She came to him and touched his feet. This was the Hindu way- she had seen her Hindu friends do it. "No, no, no, you must not touch my feet, daughters are Lakshmi- they must not touch anyone's feet." he exclaimed. Then he looked at her face and received a jolt. She was the carbon copy of Revati- same height, same facial features, same complexion. It seemed as if someone had created a wax replica of his granddaughter- only this was no wax replica but a living girl.

"Who are you, my child?" he asked her gently.

"May I speak to you alone?" she said.

"I am very busy, can't you tell me here?"

"It is about the Kumbh Mela" she said softly. Just then Gajanan came with a sheaf of papers and seeing the girl was transfixed to the spot.

"Impossible, impossible" he murmured softly.

"Gajanan, let us go to my room. Call our daughter-in-law also and let us talk to this child."

Painfully he rose from the sofa and was helped to go inside by his son. Reshma followed, dazed by the splendor of the home and the way life was turning for her. They came to the room and Reshma saw a much older version of herself- "Amma" she said and ran to the lady. Like her husband, the lady was dumbstruck and some motherly instinct made her put her arms around the girl.

The old gentleman sat down and saw to it that the door was shut. "Yes my dear, you mentioned Kumbh mela."

"You must be my Dadaji," Reshma's lips trembled and tears fell. "I am the unfortunate baby that was stolen."

Now the husband rushed to his wife who held the girl to her and was sobbing and he would have wept too, soft hearted as he was when "Gajanan!"- was called sharply by the old seth.

"Yes father!"

"Bring the child to me first" he said.

The crying girl went to him and knelt in front of him.

"Now tell me, how did you know about us and also tell me, my child where you are living and what you are called."

Reshma fearfully told her entire story, including her convent education, kathak , mujras, Nusrat Jahan and Hamida Khala's role in getting her to know about the past.

She also told him about Atif who was sleeping in the next room in the hotel.

"Bapuji what shall we do?" his daughter-in-law asked.

"What is there to be done? Our lost child has come back to us, our Gomati has come back to us so there will be double celebrations. Gajanan! Tell Shiboo Bhai that another Navratan set must be crafted immediately so my Gomati can wear it. Call all the family members, relatives, servants. Let me declare to all that my lost granddaughter has been found."

"But Dadaji my past?" Reshma asked fearfully.

"That is gone. Miyan Atif will be sent back to Lucknow with instructions that if Nusrat Jahan opens her mouth she will be silenced. As for the kind Hamida we will keep her in some good pension."

"Bapuji, suppose Rewati's in-laws find out about her past and break the marriage?" the mother asked.

"If they are cowardly enough to do so then so be it, we will be lucky to have nothing to do with such a low family then."

Reshma, now Gomati, heard all this with pure bliss – could life turn about like this for her? She would get her respectability and security and her family! "Allah be praised" she said.

"Bhagwan ka lakh lakh shukr hai" said her mother.

"It is all the same" said Seth Dhanpat Rai.

THIRTEEN

Letters From Kargil

Letter one

Dearest Ganga,

You have written how hot it is at home these days. Here the mountain peaks are covered with snow. Wherever I see there is snow all around-even the trenches are covered with it. Yes, I have got the pullover you knitted for me. They provide real warmth in such trying times. The peaches and plums would have ripened by now at home in the fields.

Things are getting better now. When we had just come, we sometime thought that the enemy was the incarnation of the "Rakta Beej".Do you remember Baba would tell stories about the demon whose drops of blood created more and more demons. Now we are getting better control over our enemies. I am sorry to stop now. I have just now received a message to report for action.

Love,
Ram

Letter Two

Dearest Ganga,

I was very uneasy yesterday. One can tell such things only to one's wife, and you, my dear, are the most understanding wife I could have ever asked for. We do not fear death, but we really dread being captured and mercilessly tortured. There were twenty of us and as we inched our way, we found that we were surrounded. Abdullah was giving me his amulet to hand over to his wife. But the situation that the enemy was on our land brought out anger and with it even greater courage. Then it was our day.

As I am lying in my tent, the wind howls like a crazed animal, and I long to have you near me. When I come home, the first thing you make is kheer. What is growing in the backyard? How are you managing your fronts at home? How are you looking after our son, the fields, the kitchen and cattle? Ah! You are the brave wife of a fauji!

Lots of Love,
Ram

Letter three

Dearest Ganga,

Why were you crying so much over the phone? It was difficult to control myself then. Next time we get a chance to phone, tell me about home. Do not ever cry. Our hills which have intruders, I consider as our cornfields where weeds also crop up. We go from field to field cleaning out weeds and here we go from peak to peak cleaning out those intruders. Much has been cleared.

You have always laughed at my romantic nature- "A soldier and romantic!' You would say. It can't be helped. Yesterday when I was climbing a high peak, hidden under the snow I saw a violet in full bloom! How it must have struggled to survive and bloom! You, my wife, are like that violet. So I plucked it and put it in my pocket and when I come, I will put it in your palm.

Yours,
Ram

Letter Four

Dearest Ganga,

We passed some villages yesterday. Though most had left but some brave ones had stayed behind. They gave us thick corn rotis with saag and then tea with a lot of milk and ginger. It reminded me so much of home. I don't know why but they treated us like heroes.

Tomorrow we have to go on a special mission. We cannot write the names of such places in our letters. I am sure we will be as successful as we have been in the past.

Don't worry about me, Shoolini Mata will look after me. I am wearing her locket, obeying your orders! But, sometimes I worry what will happen to you if I am no more. You are so young and beautiful.

My commander has sent the medicines for Mother's illness and our unit's medical team will visit our village after all this is over. Then Baba's cataract can be operated upon.

Does Munna ask about me?

Yours ever,
Ram

Letter Five

Dearest Ganga,

I don't know if this letter will ever reach you. We are surrounded. There are only a few of us left here. We are well hidden and awaiting the right moment to strike. I thought of writing a few lines to you.

The land on the north -west side is ours. If our neighbors create problems, go to any officer in the D.C office, I am sure he will help. In case you forget, there is Rs. 42,000 in the bank. It is my dream that Munna should join the army.

Do not go alone to reap the harvest near the jungle side. Always take somebody along. If you would not have married me Ashok would have been a very good husband. He is still a bachelor. I feel

To
Smt. Ganga Gazta
Village- Devghat
Dist.- Solan
Himachal Pradesh

Regret to inform that Lance Nayak Ram Gazta was killed in action. Articles on his person are as follows-

Letters - 5 nos.
Locket- 1 no.
Wallet- 1 no.
Dried Flower – 1 no.

FOURTEEN

Daughters of Eve

They came to the new colony when a couple of people had well settled there. That there were very beautiful daughters in the family was discovered by a group of children who just stood and gaped at them. The girls were sunning themselves and their wet hair reached their ankles. Well nearly their ankles. They were very fair, rosy and had lovely expressive features. A four- year-old who was watching took the lollipop out of her mouth to ask her elder sister all of six years "Are they fairies?" "They are our new Bengali neighbors" she was told.

They were the first Bengalis to settle in that colony and with them grew a myth- at least in the minds of the younger generation that all Bengali women were very beautiful. They were three of them. "I have five daughters." Their mother smiled and said "and three sons. The sons are settled and two of the girls are married, we hope to get as good husbands for these too," GOOD husbands! Great Heavens! A whole army of eligible bachelors would line up to their door- thought the ladies of the colony.

Though the colony was small and the residents few, but as it usually happened in such cases, the grapevine was an especially strong and flourishing one; the biggest link were the two women who sold vegetables to these families. Carrying a huge basket of seasonal vegetables on their heads, they would go from door to door and collect all the gossip as well. So when Lalmani (the first seller) casually dropped the information that the Choudhary boy was a frequent visitor at the new home, the colony was abuzz with speculations. The Choudhary boy was a "ne'er do well" sort, somehow managing to pass each class, more interested in pretty girls than in his books, and it was generally predicted about him that he would bring grief to his parents. So, when the vegetable- seller brought this news, many do-gooders thought of fulfilling their duty and advising Mrs. Ganguli about the matter.

Mrs. Ganguli was quite surprised to see ladies coming to her house quite frequently and advising her but it never came to her that the regular visits of the Choudhary boy would be harmful. And when the most vocal lady of the colony, Mrs. Nair stated in no uncertain terms the reason why the boy visited her family, she took it with a pinch of salt. Then one could see the fellow shopping for Mrs. Ganguli, seeing off her mother to the station, paying their electricity bill, even taking Mrs. Ganguli's woollens to the dry cleaners. A certain charm had crept in his way of conversation, he was more polite to the ladies, even wishing them at times, and wonder of wonders; he even managed to pass his BA with a second class. The colony ladies felt that he was a transformed being and all due to Manjula. But could their marriage take place? According to the dictates of Custom, it could not, one was a Bengali Brahmin, the other a Maithil Brahmin- Brahmin, no doubt, but from other communities! But was it nothing that Mr. Choudhary was considered a shrewd businessman? Amidst all this turmoil this couple kept a stiff upper lip and soon it was heard that the boy had a very good job in Assam. (The father's contacts were very helpful) he departed soon and some ladies swore to the tearful farewell held in the Ganguli drawing room. The gossip died only to crop up with a vengeance when Mrs. Choudhary herself stepped out of her white Ambassador and delivered a wedding card at each home- "Anand is getting married next week, we got such a gem of a girl, a typical Mithilanchal beauty, and my dears, Anand took to her at once."

The colony was aghast. But knowing the shrewd Choudharys, they felt it was bound to happen, and one day the bride came, radiantly beautiful. Manjula attended the wedding and looked as radiant, but Mrs. Nair swore that she had wiped her eyes behind the jasmine bushes.

Then came Shekhar. He was the very righteous Mrs. Verma's son. You see, he just went to borrow the class notes from Manjula, he had been ill and so had not attended some classes, moreover, what are class mates for? Shekhar had not even sipped the tea placed in front of him when Mrs. Mishra huffing and puffing, rang his mother's door bell, notifying her of the events. She had merely come to borrow a pinch of baking soda and then very casually dropped the news. The righteous lady turned out to be smarter and said that she herself had sent her son there for he needed the notes and poor boy, he was so shy, he had to be pushed to go anywhere, not like some whom she knew whose sons came only to eat and sleep at home. The tale bearer winced; her own son was among them. But she was quite satisfied when her neighbor told her that her neighbor said that when the poor boy had returned, there was a bitter quarrel between mother and son.

Then came the long list of Ravis, and Ramakants and Udayans and Vikrams but there were no takers. Mrs. Ganguli was soon named as 'Bahama Mama', upon whom a very popular song was based. The lady in the song had six very beautiful daughters and suitors came by the dozens, but all left puzzled, not knowing which one to choose, each was so lovely.

Manjula passed her MA and took up lectureship in her own college, it was said that when she entered class, the attendance was double as students of other subjects came to sit and stare at her. The younger Manjusha and the youngest Boola were still studying.

Those were the days when girls were married off just as they passed school, some modern parents even let their daughters complete BA, but to complete MA and take up a job and still stay free was something far too daring. Tongues wagged and the girl felt very uncomfortable in the vicinity of the dozen pairs of eyes that followed her in the colony. She asked for a transfer and got it. Delhi was much more conducive for her and slowly people started forgetting her. Then one day the folks saw Mrs. Ganguli resplendent in her red-bordered tussore silk, distributing wedding cards, "Its Manjula's isn't it?" all asked eagerly. The brilliance of the smile dimmed, " It's Manjusha's." Remember the Chakravortys who had the bicycle factory? Their fourth daughter's brother-in-law's third cousin's eldest son is an engineer in Bokaro, he is the groom."

Typical of the colony ladies, all joined in the merry making and the wedding preparations. Cooks and other help were hired but could the colony ladies be far behind? They came and assisted in dicing the mountain of vegetables. Mrs. Nair, though the most vocal, was the swiftest and the house was decorated by the elder boys and girls. And when the barat came, all the men folk of the colony came to welcome them and there was a confusion among the baratis whether all those standing at the gate were the bride's own uncles.

Manjusha looked divine and the little girls who sat around her exclaimed at her sari and jewelry and the ladies at her beauty. "She looked more beautiful than Durga," said the righteous Mrs. Verma, looking askance at her own daughter-in-law, for poor Shekhar's wife was quite plain.

There was a missing chord- there was no Manjula. "She could not make it," Basanti explained. She was the eldest and a mother of four. "She had to take some college girls on an excursion." "She could not stand her sister getting married before her," hissed Mrs. Choudhary who had not forgiven the Anand affair. Manjula remained an enigma.

Now there was only Boola in the large white house with the green shutters. Well, she was the greatest beauty of all. Her champa complexion, her satin skin, her doe-like eyes, her ankle length hair, she even had a rich and melodious voice to accompany them. It seemed as if the mother had poured all her skills and talent into this youngest of hers, bequeathing all that she had received from the Maker. This girl could crochet the finest of laces; embroider a bouquet of flowers so realistically that one was tempted to sniff it. And she could cook the best fish in mustard sauce in the whole region. True, only the luckiest would get her.

Eligible bachelors started beating a path to her door, only to be rejected. And when the debonair Ashim Banerjee, an M. Tech from Massachussets, a green car holder mind you, and oh so handsome, when he started crooning Tagore songs in his Hemant Kumar voice, even Mrs. Nair smiled in her backyard while hanging out the wash. "They will make a wonderful couple," was the verdict of the whole colony. But Ashim went alone to USA, heartbroken, swore all romantics, Boola did not care a fig for him. "Which Greek god will come down to earth for her?" sneered the vitriolic Mrs. Verma who had introduced Ashim to that family.

Boola went on rejecting suitors and most of them married and had children while she remained unattached. Poor Mr. Ganguli died of brain thrombosis and all said his end could have been more peaceful had "the wretch" married.

It was another June evening when the very air around a person breathed fire and dark clouds would roll in the sky bringing false hopes of cool showers only to be blown away by the stinging wind, when Mrs. Ganguli could be seen with a sheaf of wedding cards, accompanied by Basanti and Paroma, the elder ones. "Is it for Manjula?" all enquired. "No" Paroma said in her sprightly way. "Manjula is too engrossed in her career to think of marriage, little Boola is to be wedded." Boola, the icy hearted one, then all remembered how it was on a summer evening that Ashim had sung about the statue of stone which he could endow with feelings only if given a chance, and how that high and mighty miss had given a toss to her long braids and had walked inside. Mrs. Lele who was coming from the store had actually seen it,

"Is it Ashim?" all asked eagerly. "No, it's a man who works in her office," Basanti informed.

And thus, the last of Bahama Mama's daughters was married. But what about Manjula you ask. She came to the wedding accompanied by a lanky, bearded, Khadi- clad professor of Anthroplogy whom she had married in a registry office a week ago. That was Manjula, completely original and so very independent. Needless to say, she immediately became the role model for the younger set of girls in the colony.

But, what about Ashim Banerjee? He visits India every June and in the hot evenings as one goes by his garden which is carefully screened off with juhi creepers and jasmine bushes, one can hear the deep, melodious notes and the mournful songs of Tagore issue forth- "Ashar Sandhya"-. No, he did not marry.

FIFTEEN

Bhanumati and Her Charges

Bhanumati herded her charges through the traffic, assigning duties all the while. There were six of them, all of varying sizes and unless one kept a sharp lookout, one would shirk work or worse, be kidnapped. Most were still too young to know any better, and if they shirked work there would be less food in the evening, not that they demanded more from her but if they extended their plates and she could not refill them, she felt horrid. It was not an easy life but then it was better than the lives of many she had seen and she had shuddered inwardly and had vowed to die before she became their sort.

A redline bus blocked the way and when the girls crossed from front the driver and conductor cracked an obscene joke and laughed raucously. They were quite harmless if one was in a crowd. She was glad they had been allowed the route near the Inter State Bus Terminus, ISBT, which they called "bus adda". In this profession one was allotted a place, area by payment of some money to the dadas. They were some who did not pay yet carried on their work and had to face the wrath of the dadas, some simply disappeared. She had to ration the food at times when the business was not good but they never protested.

She saw to it that Ritu began work- she was very shy and had to be pushed nearly every day, she had the busiest area, the front of the ISBT, where business was easy and plentiful yet she would hesitate, may be as she came from such a different background. Bhanumati never enquired from where her girls came, never probed about their past- what was the point? The important thing was the present, moreover the less one knew about them the easier it was to make them mingle in the group. She herself remembered so little about herself- Old Chachi and this dilapidated old hut- nothing else. When the old woman was struck with paralysis it was natural for Bhanumati to take over, and she did, shy at first, but with experience developed a thicker hide, a brazen attitude.

Then Rehana had come. Nobody knew who her father was and as her mother had just then died of leprosy nobody wanted her. She had stood quietly at the door of Bhanumati's hovel and had been asked inside- she never left after that. Roshni, they had found crying piteously near a gutter, hardly of two years- but Bhanumati, all of ten years had foresight and had realized that she would be good for business even now and after she grew, be even more useful. They called her Roshni as after she came, the municipality lit the backlanes of that area and some light entered their hovel too. Suniti's mother married again after her father died- most probably the step-father was a devil so she came to Bhanumati. When the old woman died, Bhanumati's brood totalled five- Suniti had brought her younger sister Sumati also and at the age of twelve, Bhanumati found herself the head of the business. The old woman had coached her in the tricks of the trade so she knew how to make the most of the situation. She had five years' experience now in her line and had established a good reputation- that of a just and caring person. It came naturally, when all handed their earnings to her she had to be fair and it was her responsibility that they were fed, clothed, looked after in illness and protected. She was also known to pay the dadas right on time. So when the dada gave her the charge of Ritu, she was not surprised. He trusted her- even hinted that he had been paid well by the stepmother to have her removed. They must have been rich- the way the girl talked and ate showed it.

She saw Rim and Jhim sidling up to her, what was the matter? Rim and Jhim were twins, very fair and pretty and they sang well too. They too had a cruel step-mother who was barren and felt threatened by the girls. One day when their father was away she put them on a train and got down when the train was moving. The girls were spotted by Bhanumati near Kashmere Gate

And she took them in. They were christened Rim and Jhim as she found them when it was raining. They brought her good money for they could coax, cajole, wheedle and sing till the one approached parted with some coins.

This profession of beggary has its own hazards. She taught the girls to beg, coax, tell sob stories but keep their distance. She never let them stand singly at their post and no matter how far she might wander away kept an eagle eye on her charges, woe be tide the person who dared touch any one of them- she knew the choicest of abuses and let out a volley of them at the top of her voice. "What is it?" she asked Rim. "Didi, we are hungry". Oh, that was all, she had feared worse. Yes, this was also business- you had to plan, work accordingly, persevere, face losses and make profits also. She took out some coins and told the twins to buy a bun each.

Once Rim Jhim had followed a group of pilgrims and sang bhajans; when Bhanumati saw from a distance that they were interested, she sent Ritu to join them- the girl knew many shlokas and could chant them musically,. That was a day to remember. Each person of the group had rewarded them generously and the day's earnings had far exceeded her expectations. "Didi, buy chicken today" they all had clamored and she had given them a nice feast. She also set aside some money to buy Roshni a second hand frock, the tattered one showed too much- the rest of the money she buried in a hole in the hovel.

The best part of the day was evening, when the day's work was done and all would trudge home. They would take out their earnings from the various recesses in their clothes and hand it over to her. She would count it, and set aside the money needed to buy fuel, flour and vegetables. After eating they would spread their mats and lie down and after the hard work all would soon be asleep.

Today as she stir-fried the vegetables Rehana reminded her "Didi, tomorrow we will have to change our route- its 15th August." Oh! She had nearly forgotten! She smiled at the girl-"Good that you reminded me we must tell the others." Rehana was a very good assistant, may be after she retired Rehana would manage- but why should she retire? What would she do? She would often daydream if she had enough money she would start a small shop of her own. There would be glass doors and windows and everything would shine and sparkle and she would sell things to eat. Then she scolded herself- what foolishness to dream of such things, might as well plan for tomorrow.

After the meal she spoke sternly to them-"As the place is not very familiar, we must keep together, if people do not pay immediately, don't run after them, the crowd will be huge, you will get lost. Keep away from policemen." She worried about Rim and Jhim they were so pretty they immediately attracted unwelcome attention. "Is fifteenth August a Hindu festival or Muslim?" Roshni asked, she was six now and curious about everything. They had all laughed and Ritu spoke quietly- "It's for the whole country- a festival of all religions." This led to more questions, or answers and laughter and would have continued if Farhana Bi the doormat seller had not shouted at them from the next hut- "Nasty beggars, one cannot even sleep due to them."

Why does Lal Qila change so much on this day, Bhanumati often wondered. It would look so much different from the usually friendly building that provided so much space for beggars and hawkers. Today one only saw policemen, in uniform, out of it, on the street, behind the bushes, all of them tense. Bhanumati gathered her brood around her and was deciding the best place for business when she and the girls were roughly jostled and pushed inside the bamboo barricades, and two policemen came up instantly-'Sit down' they ordered.

"Didi, we will have to stay here now till the mela is over, we will not be able to earn anything," Rehana said quietly. "Bad luck, that's what we are having, sit down until it's over." Roshni promptly fell asleep and even Bhanumati started dozing, only Ritu's eyes were wide open drinking in everything. "Didi, look the Prime Minister!" she had whispered tugging at the elder girl's sleeve, "Oh, this one, I have seen his picture many times," Jhim said. The old gentleman started speaking and the crowd fell silent. After sometime the children started getting restless. "Let's go," Roshni said loudly and was hit sharply by a baton. Bhanumati rose angrily, "Look at those school children, how they are talking and laughing! You will not say anything to them, but you will hit us as we are poor!"

Heads turned and she saw a man and a woman looking at them closely. She sat down wearily. Just then she heard the very familiar "garibi", and sat up. What was the gentleman saying? She heard that free meals would be given to all school children, all over the country. This way he said that the poorest of the poor would be provided for, the citizens of tomorrow would be nourished; children would not go hungry. Poorest of the poor! She wanted to laugh. If those who could go to school were the poorest, then what would she and her girls be called? Which class did they belong to? Those who went to school had a home, parents, who would somehow provide, but who looked after her sort? Here she was worrying her heart out that she had to sit behind these barricades and could not beg, what would she put in the plates that the girls would place expectantly in a row? Did the old gentleman know that there were so many of her sort? May be he did not know.

"Let's leave, didi, all are going." Ritu's words shook her from a trance and as she shuffled towards the exit, she felt a deep resentment towards those who could go to school. "Didi, don't you think we all could go to school? The Municipality school is so near our home, we could study and get our food too." Ritu pleaded. "For that you need a proper home, books, uniform, do you think they will admit beggars?" Ritu's face fell but it was necessary to be cruel to be kind sometimes. Just then a young couple, right in front of them turned to look. The woman was very pretty and smiled at them-"Do you want to go to school?" she asked.

Years of experience had taught Bhanumati to be wary of the rich – such would never put anything in their bowls but would look at her as if she were dirt. Bhanumati started shuffling away. "Wait," this time the young man spoke. There was something kindly about him, his face had such an honest look and his voice so soothing that the girl stopped-the brood also stopped. Sensing something was taking place, all the girls instinctively gathered around her. "O master we are seven" murmured the woman. "Are you sisters?" he asked. "Yes," she said better not reveal too much. "My wife and I have a small organization in which we help children like you. We heard what you were saying, you don't have to beg all your lives. We will send you to school and you can stay in the home we have for children like you. In return you must work – do small jobs. "What kind of jobs?" Bhanumati asked suspiciously. "Cleaning, cooking and after school you must learn a craft, some special work which will bring you money." "If we don't like it we will come back," "Of course!" he smiled.

Bhanumati looked at the eager faces around her and remembered the indignities, the hunger, the uncertainty they all had to face and there was no way out. Here was a chance, why not give it a try? If so, then going back to the hut would be folly. If the dada got to know she was leaving with the girls, he would prevent her, her departure meant losing a good chunk of regular income. "Can we come now?" she asked. Both of them laughed and he beckoned. They followed him. There was an old jeep into which they all clambered. Bhanumati's business mind was racing fast. What did they have to lose? If these people put them in a school and taught them a decent way to earn their living, it would be a dream come true. If they were cheated, she would run away with the girls, she knew all the tricks, nobody could stop her.

The man was asking their names and Roshni, always starved for love, sat close to the woman and despite the grime and the lice the woman was patting her. Rim and Jhim were smiling, Sumati and Suniti were sitting quietly but Rehana looked questioningly at her. The elder girl smiled assuringly.

A noise of something hitting against the jeep and clattering to the road made the man turn. "Did something fall?" he asked.

"Nothing much, only my begging bowl." Bhanumati answered.

SIXTEEN

A Little Courage

She stood shivering at the bus stop. The jacket was thick but the leggings were not and she pulled her cap lower. There was no sign of the bus; and it grew more lonely. The occasional cars swept her in their head lights and she turned her head askance to avoid their glare. A rickshaw passed, she pitied that man who was sniffing continuously- he bent towards her- "Chalna hai didi" she shook her head- home was so far! And this metropolis was so unkind- so friendless! Now had it been her Manipur, she would have long found somebody to go with, or someone to take her home. But this city without a soul! She remembered the reasons why she had to come, gritted her teeth and paced the bus stop. The bus had to come soon.

She saw the headlights of some bikes coming- may be three men on one and their raucous laughter and cowered behind a pillar. She hoped they would not notice her., and flattened herself against the wall and pillar, hiding her face. They did not zoom past, rather they stopped at a distance and started their crazy antics- doing all sorts of tricks on the wide road- another biker had parked and was standing on the seat and dancing, the whiskey bottle pouring a continuous stream in his open mouth. The others too had bottles that they started breaking one after the other on the street- the broken pieces of glass flying around like shrapnel. NO BUS! She was terrified.

Just then she saw a car passing, the man behind the wheel saw her and slowed. He was middle aged and had a kindly look. He was alone. The shouting and drunken laughter became louder. A bottle fell close by. Then one of them seeing her gleefully shouted-"Ladki, ladki hai." Before she could realize what she was doing, she ran to the slowing car and wrenched open the door, sat and the car sped on, leaving a trail of glass and obscenities.

"Where do you have to go?"

She got her breath back, "Mahipalpur".

"That's far but I will drop you."

"You came just in time." She said gratefully.

"Yes, that was sheer coincidence."

So, he sounded educated. Good English, showed a good background, he was safe, she decided.

"Where do you work?"

"I am a receptionist."

He spoke in his cell phone-"Same place."

"Was it your wife?" She asked. He gave a short laugh. Her bones ached and she was lulled to a semi- stupor by the warmth of the car. Suddenly she felt that the roads were unfamiliar.

"Listen, do you know which road to take? This looks unfamiliar!"

He gave another short laugh. She started feeling fear creeping from her legs and creating a hollow in her stomach.

The words of the police came to her- Do not take lifts from strangers.

"Please stop the car. I will take a bus." He stopped the car.

It was dark and desolate all around. She could make out bushes and a long stretch of lonely road. Dark shapes sprang up from nowhere and a strong palm pushed her back into the car. The scream that rose to her lips was cut short by a strong cigarette smelling palm that tried to mash her lips. She tried to clamp her teeth on the palm and for a second he released her and slapped her hard, twice, across the mouth.

"She fights. Show some spirit, we enjoy a fight." It was the driver whom she had thought to be kind, to be safe.

Her jacket was unzipped by someone who tried to grope her flailing body, for yes, she would not lie supine, she would fight. She kicked out at the restraining hands around her ankles. May be she'd reached a vulnerable spot for she heard an obscenity and the lashes of a belt. Oh God! The pain tore through her body as he whipped her. Then he was pushed aside, her leggings torn away and then she felt pain and more pain as her body was violated again and again.

"From where does Rajneesh pick them up? It was good and it was free." She heard the chuckles as she was made to sit and then pushed out where she stumbled in the bushes. Her legs were bare, her jacket thrown across her body. Her head had hit a stone when they had pushed her in the bushes and with the throbbing she could feel something wet trickling down her forehead. Her thighs were wet- blood and their muck. Now she lay supine. She groped in the grass for her cell phone- she'd call her room mates but she could neither find her bag nor her phone.

Shock hit her in waves and she gulped the air and short screams, animal- like in their agony came out.

"Kaun hai, arey koi hai?"

Someone called out. She could make out the shape of a bicycle no, two bicycles- men, oh not again!

But this time the arms were kind. The bare legs were covered by a chadar. She was made to sit up gently and a lota of water was pressed to her lips. She drank, some kind heart said, "oh oh", someone was talking on the phone, headlights flashed, then she sank into oblivion.

She was in the hospital. Someone was swabbing between her legs, then thighs. "Yes, rape and assault", she heard. She could feel the sting of some medicine on her forehead. A salwar was provided. Next time she regained her senses, she found herself at the police station. There were uniforms all around. Were they leering? Men again! Oh not again! And suddenly she heard a strong feminine voice- "Don't crowd around her, let her breathe for God's sake." A uniform! Trousers! But no, the face was of a woman, thank the lord for this mercy.

"Can you speak now?"

She nodded.

"But maybe you'd like a cup of tea first. Arre, chai lao."

A hot glass was thrust in her cold fingers and as the warmth spread through her body, she started crying pitifully.

"Stop that immediately!" the kind voice had turned fierce. "Be strong! tell us the details and we will see that justice is done- whoever they are."

The information came out in jerks, snatches, bits and as she came to the part that when she heard good English she thought she was safe, the lady said "Huh" with derision "It's that type, in day time sugar will not melt in their mouths, they think that they can get away with anything because of their money and backing – those wolves in sheep's clothing. But you see, we'll get them."

Saying it was easy. In the morning the "site" was revisited and she recovered her phone and her bag. Her friends were notified, she went home. She took a week's leave from work, the body and mind needed healing. The whole day she would lie in bed, under her quilt, her body racked by sobs. The fear that they would come again filled her with such dread that she feared stepping out of the house.

There was a sharp knock at the door. She froze. The knocking was persistent. She dived into the quilt and covered her ears. Now with the knocking she heard "Police". She crept to the door and peeped through the spy hole. Oh! it was the same lady police officer! She opened the door with relief and was embarrassed to see that the room looked very messy.

"So you were hiding?" the lady police officer smiled. "Can we have a cup of tea?"

She rushed to set two cups of tea, luckily her room mate had left milk, bearing a tray of marie biscuits and tea she went to the lady. Her name she saw was Amita Grewal and she was an IPS, must be senior SP she guessed.

"So, Dolma, do you feel better now?" hearing her name on the police woman's lips made Dolma feel good, as if she were a part of her life too.

"But I feel very scared. They are not yet caught, are they?" she asked

"No child, we have not been successful so I have come to you, you have to be a part of our plan."

"What plan?"

"You will be used as a decoy. You will stand again at that place at the same time. I am sure that he will come again. Old habits die hard. We will be in the bushes. As soon as you recognize him, engage him in conversation, we will take care of the rest."

Dolma's hands shook as she heard these words. Face them again!

As if she could read her mind, Amita Grewal said, "Don't be afraid, I will be very close by. This is the only way to trap them. Help us, they must be caught." Reluctantly Dolma agreed. A date and time was fixed.

It was the same bus stop. Same time. Was it the same wind that blew her hair all over her face, nearly toppling her by its ferocity? They waited till 10 p.m. then Amita Grewal called it a day. "Too late for him, we'll try tomorrow. She stood there for seven days. The eighth day they struck it lucky.

This time there were no rowdy bikers so she could have a feel that the canary yellow Mercedez moving closer was his, she was sure! The heel of her shoe had caught in the door and she had scraped it- she saw in the street light that there was a long mark there. She smiled at him- come into my parlour said the spider to the fly- only this time she would be the spider. He stopped the car. "You again? Listen I must apologise for the little roughness but it was fun, wasn't it?"

She smiled and nodded and motioned behind her back. Just as he opened the door for her he was immediately surrounded by policemen led by their SP Amita Grewal.

Watching the lady in action provided the greatest catharsis for Dolma. She dragged him out by his collar- he was over six feet- she much less than that but ferocity, dexterity and the element of surprise were on her side. The beating that he got on the road was just the beginning.

"Oh! You'll sing in the police station and tell us of your accomplices," she threatened.

All were arrested. A fast track court gave them seven years imprisonment (RI) and a hefty fine that was not difficult for them to pay as all came from affluent families. Many spanners were put in the functioning of the court but Dolma and Amita were successful.

"A little courage, Dolma, and that helped a lot,"- Amita said as she patted the girl good bye.

SEVENTEEN

Thus are the Great Made

Neha Saraogi looked around Parliament House, quiet, stately, dignified, surrounded with greenery, flowers all over. Success should not make her complacent. From the valley of Kashmir, plains of Bihar to the coastal areas of the southern states, she had traveled everywhere, unearthed stories that shocked, brought tears to the sensitive and stupefied the rest to silence. And here she was today, to reveal to the masses the true face of the leaders they had elected. The members would start arriving shortly.

Just then a white Ambassador entered. She nodded to the cameraman and rushed to meet the Finance Minister. He gave her a curt nod-she smiled back and was assailed by a blast of perfume as the beauties of Parliament, two former actresses climbed the steps. They gave her a sunny smile. The RJD supremo was next. "What is your message to the common man sir,?" she gushed. "Khao piyo, mast raho" he said in his typical rustic manner. The opposition group was next followed by representatives from Haryana and Punjab. Neha followed them inside. Today was the first day of the monsoon session.

The session began. She could hear the speaker rumble monotonously-"It is the duty of this house to discuss subjects that are generally complex and sometimes contentious. But I hope and believe that a frank expression of opinions may assist us to understand each other and to appreciate one another`s point of view. At the same time I am confident that I may count upon you, ladies and gentlemen, to assist me in maintaining the high standards of dignity and courtesy that has hitherto characterized the proceedings of this House, worthy of the high traditions of the assembly."

Neha saw the FM rise, seek permission to begin the debate that would move the bill granting 33 percent reservation for women in Parliament as well as various elected bodies. She focused carefully. The FM wore moon-like spectacles that gave him an owlish appearance, but his diction was perfect. Neha tried to concentrate on what he was saying-"A large mass of women continue to lack spokepersons who understand their problems and are committed to their cause. Greater participation of women will help direct the rate and type of changes in the general status of women. Given such a scenario,33% reservation for women in various elected bodies becomes imperative,"

A beauty queen of not-so yester years got up to make her point. Adjusting the folds of her sari, she patted her hair, looked around and giving a seductive smile began-"Such measures are required for bringing about a change in the minds of the people to break the traditional attitude which inhibit most women from articulating their problems and participating in their own affairs."

Neha was surprised to see that even before she could begin her next sentence the Home Minister rose and glowered at her. She remembered that once in a candid moment in an interview he had mentioned, off the record, that she was in college with him and was a graduate only due to his notes. The HM started without any formalities or niceties-"How can it improve the lot of women? Would it not amount to giving more power to men who will manipulate their wives to seek tickets on reserved seats? Can social evils like bride burning be stopped by having more women in Parliament? Instead of doing anything positive, which requires a great deal of effort, we have resorted to cosmetic measures."

"Oh yes, I do agree with you," chimed a sweet thing newly elected, "cosmetics must be made tax free so that they are easily available to all women!" She looked around her, bewildered by the ensuing laughter and wrapped her chiffon sari tightly around her. As the laughter died down, the RJD supremo yawned and spoke-"This matter is of no importance, only waste of time". Pat came the reply from the earlier beauty-"Shall we discuss the fodder scam then?" The wily man who chose to show himself as a country bumpkin appealed to the Speaker-"Hon`ble sir, this is unfair! They call me tainted but I appeal to god to make the earth swallow me if---"

"For that you will have to go to the roads of your state where you can disappear in any pothole the roads are filled with!" retorted the beauty queen amidst shouts of laughter.

"Madam," said the man" I am a great admirer of your exceptional beauty, I promise that I will make the roads of my state as smooth as your cheeks". In the raucous laughter that issued from a particular section, the actress rose, fuming-"I take exception to such a remark"

The speaker intervened with-"Personal attributes as a general rule, should not be commented upon."-

After the chaos, the minister for Tourism, known for her exuberance, daring ideas and westernized ways, rose. As usual she was wearing a designer sari. "I believe that a law should be made that every family must have a girl child. If a girl is not conceived, she should be adopted. Many crimes can be curbed if we change our thinking about the girl child being a burden. Woman, the maker of man, needs no reservation. Hum se hai zamana, zamane se hum nahin". She sat in thunderous applause, more because of the couplet, Neha thought, because she found many of the clappers were dozing earlier, the couplet had roused them!

The beauty queen, still smarting under the earlier comment now stood-"We have certain politicians who put their wives in their places when corruption charges against them begin to hurt. This is without reservation." in the ensuing laughter and table- pounding, the gentleman in question arose-"I protest against this attack, a direct one against me and my wife."

The Beauty Queen was on her feet again-"Yours is a singular case the only example in our country! How disgusting!"

As if on cue, the minister for tourism stood-"And look at the earthen cups-his kulhars he has started on the trains. How unhygienic -!How uncultured!"

The country bumpkin was totally incensed now. "Uncultured! This is high culture! Even in ancient Indian society there was the use of nature-friendly products. What will you fashionable, convent educated ladies know-no patriotism, no feeling for the downtrodden!" The Speaker intervened-"Silence, silence! Let us remember that every member has the fullest liberty to express his own views, remembering that every other member has the same liberty. It becomes necessary therefore to exercise restraint on the content and extent as also on the language of the discussion. Please continue keeping this in mind."

Just then the MP from Punjab got up with a "Sat sri akal to all" without waiting further he started "Punjab has as much right of 60 percent on the Ganga- Yamuna link waters as Haryana has 40 percent right on other rivers of Punjab. Under the 60-40 ratio, Haryana is already drawing more than its share of water from Punjab. Then where is the need for an additional canal to take water to Haryana from Punjab rivers? We lift underground water for use and the water table is receding at the rate of 36-42 inches every year."

Just as heatedly an MP from Haryana shouted-"If there is no water from Punjab then Haryana will not permit entry through her roads. You remember! Coal for your thermal plants passes through Haryana! No water, no roads!"

Immediately the group from Haryana joined in, gesturing wildly-"No water, no roads" while the Punjab MP went menacingly to the Haryana MP and seizing his collar repeated-"no water, no roads". Both started grappling and soon there was a free-for –all between both parties.

"Oh what bores they are!" exclaimed the sweet little thing and made a ball out of the paper distributed to all some time before and threw it at the fighting men. The paper ball caught the Punjab MP squarely on his forehead and he retorted by piling the choicest epithets on his Haryana counterpart and giving a sock on his jaw.

Pandemonium ensued. The Speaker kept on with his "Silence, silence! ladies and gentlemen remember who you are !" and at last the final "The House is adjourned sine die."

Neha`s camera rolled on-it was a rewarding day-fights are always more interesting!

EIGHTEEN

The Table Cloth

Preparations were on for her marriage. There was a mad rush to complete all the tasks. The departments were clearly defined, the work areas explicitly distributed. Elder Sister just back from her in law's place was busy embroidering various knick knacks for the trousseau. The tea cozy was made but whoever used such stuff these days and the sweltering climate of Kolkata would certainly not require it. The dressing table sets looked delicate in their white on white crafted work and there were so many other things, pillow cases not with the ubiquitous "Good night" embroidered on it, but tactfully done roses, there was a slight argument when Grandmother told Elder Sister to embroider atleast one pillow case with a parrot pecking grapes from a vine that being auspicious, but Elder Sister being what she was, merely nodded and smiled and conveniently forgot to make it! Mother had painstakingly embroidered so many things but she felt it was not right to have five table cloths only so Elder Sister was given a large white square of cloth to embroider.

The intelligent mind set to work, the nimble fingers flew, the silks shone on the white and soon beautiful multi -colored daisies appeared on the cloth. "Didi, why didn't you use lazy daisy instead of satin stitch? Its such back breaking work!" this was a protest from the one who was to be married for she saw how overworked and stressed everyone was and there was little she could do about it.

"This will last you for quite some time and whenever you will see it you will remember me." said Elder sister.

"I don't need a table cloth to remember you," said she, the tears that were always lurking behind her eyelids threatened to pour in a deluge.

But the table cloth was a constant, devoted part of her life. It was spread on the large teak table in her room at her in laws where all could admire the dainty stitches and delicate color. When she went to Kolkata to start her married life there was initially no table. Cheerfully, her innovative nature helping her, she set two trunks on top of each other and spread the tablecloth carefully pinning the edges in right angles, it was a very nice table indeed.

There were catastrophes, once when the foolish Mrs. Nayyar put her tea cup right in the middle of a smiling daisy, leaving a stain- she'd rushed to wash it out when the lady left. The toddlers came and found the ends very entertaining to chew. Mr. Bose stubbed out his cigarette in the ashtray and some of it fell on the table cloth. She had screamed, much to the irritation of her husband who found her rather foolish at times. Later he had admonished her- "You have so many table cloths, you keep on embroidering so many, so why make a fuss of some ancient creation?" She had bit her lip to gain composure and had spoken a little defiantly-"But it was made by my Didi."

Time flew and she started taking out the table cloth only on special occasions lest it wear. Now when she told people who asked her who'd embroidered it, they would gape with astonishment for Elder sister was a very renowned and busy doctor, the stitches were not on cloth but skin, as delicate, as meticulous as ever.

Grey crept in her hair, wrinkles came, she found herself so busy in her world. Daughters married, and one day, a bundle of joy, her grandson came. Old embroidery came back to her as she opened the box and then she saw the table cloth. She picked it up and carried it to her machine, doubling it with a thin layer of foam between, a delicate cover was made for the baby, the daisies smiling just the same though a trifle more weary. Slipping her grandson between their folds she felt that the table cloth had fulfilled its task.

NINETEEN

A Day in the Life of Ashim Kumar

The alarm clock whirred and Ashim turned wearily to stop it. His eyes just wouldn't open. A persistent shaking woke him again- it was his secretary. "Ashim! You have to start work on the new film today! Hurry!" This brought him to his feet in a trice and he rushed to the bathroom while his secretary paced the floor nervously and tried to socialize with the "money bags" the producers for new films.

Ashim Kumar was the number one romantic hero of the time, the one for whom what of young hearts, even aging ones would throb! He merely had to dip his head in a typical style, put two fingers to his forehead and smile crookedly and the effect would be electric! Many women would swoon!

Within minutes he was dressed, had his energy pills, put his arms affectionately around the waiting producers and gave his secretary the "go- ahead" for screening his new assignment and off he was to the first studio.

He was late. His leading lady sat in full make up wearing her revealing top. Oh! There was a bedroom scene with her! Ghastly! Only he and a few other actors knew what a trial it was to do such a scene with her. She, who was famed as the sexiest siren of the era, at close quarters, was terrible! Anyway, he had to bear with it! The scene demanded that she strip him. He tried to look his amorous best and not worry about the impending divorce.

He tried not to look horrified as she came lurching towards him, smiling seductively she thought, but her teeth reminded him of the barracudas- hell! Why did the whole get- up give him a feeling that he was being used as a sacrificial goat for this vampire! The barracuda had pyrrhoea too and he tried to stop his breath but if he did so the kiss would not be long! And to top it all, while she was unbuttoning him, her sharp nails managed to give him a nasty scratch. Trying to be a lover boy was not easy. It was easy in the yesteryear movies when the leading lady had to only look properly demure and coy and the hero had to only gaze at her belting out lilting soulful numbers. He was not expected to bare his body (Bare his body! That reminded him- there were a few more gray hair on his chest- had to be plucked immediately!) and do all but the final act! It was not fair on a guy! Not fair at all, especially when he had to handle partners who had no sense of hygiene, did not bother about oral hygiene at all. Damn the director who started the kiss on the screen.

Thankfully the scene was over and he could ruminate over his orange juice. A particularly persistent reporter sidled in and asked "And sir, we hear your friendship is turning into a relationship with Mehbooba!" He froze and then smiled, it was good for the lover boy image- he looked in the air, tried to bring an embarrassed expression and then mumbled "lets see, lets see" hoping that it would do the trick and the next issue of the magazine would scream the headlines- 'Ashim Kumar is in love with Mehbooba!' The image would finance all their dreams.

Time to go to the next set. This was a dance scene to be done with college students, the gyrations, the leaps in the air, the bends, he might as well be careful about the slipped disc that would resurface from time to time. Anyway, here his co-dancer was a pretty startlet, rather fresh and perky and could do all the gymnastics. The set was the middle of a Mumbai street and when the starlet smiled widely at him, he could not help thinking that she could eat a banana sideways!

It was a Shiamik Davar number and would certainly not be easy. "Okay- one, two three start, bend, leap, legs stretched, flat on the ground, pick up your partner, whirl through the air, dear God! She was like a ton of bricks! Back to the ground, let your hands sail through the air, now the hair! the hair! flap it, flip it, toss it, bend your head, hands on the floor, legs in the air!"

After it was all over, huffing and puffing and limping slightly he made it to a chair and sat down, hoping no smart-pants would come to put smart-alecky questions to him. These dance sessions always reminded him how fast age was overpowering him. And that roll of fat just below the navel- it would not disappear- his gym manager said it was not fat but sagging abs and he needed to spend more time in workouts! Okay! Some day!

It was lunch time- whatever was the time of the day but his stomach protested and lunch was served. He saw the technicians tuck in the masala chicken, dipping their chapattis in the rich brown gravy and how his mouth watered and how tasteless the dry toast and clear soup was! O when would the day come that he could eat what he wanted and to his fill! He longed to sit on the floor and join their rows and ask for the delicious yellow rice as well. He did. All hell would break lose if this continued but oh well, once in a while it was permitted!

The last shooting for the day was on the railway tracks. He, along with his leading lady, a lissome lass, had to dance on top of a moving train along with a group. When the director had earlier told him of it, his hair had risen on its ends; the terrain was treacherous, the train would be moving; and the prancing on that….oh well, he had been persuaded by the director that such is the stuff hits are made of so he had reluctantly agreed.

He climbed on the roof. He was wearing jeans but his leading lady was wearing a heavy ghagra which would bunch between her knees during the steps. At a particular point he had to hold her by the waist and dance along and just then the train took a sharp curve and they had nearly plummeted to the ground had some other dancers not caught hold of them. He was breathless and perspiring and it was all due to the fear that he may fall off. Just as he felt that all was over, the train was moving slowly and the last steps were to be done, there came the actress's possessive and jealous husband, arms akimbo, glowering at him. Palms sweating, he held her waist nevertheless trying not to remember the nasty encounter with him the last time.

The dance was over, the train halted and he manfully jumped down only to be accosted by the most jealous male of the species. "So, back to your tricks again," he started and immediately two cameras came in action as two reporters excitedly stepped in. "Are you going to fight over this?" asked one brainless male and he got a sock on the jaw. This distracted him and Ashim walked away gratefully into his waiting car. No time for formalities with the director, they'd be seen to next day. There was the CM's party to attend and hopefully the tailor would have delivered his black "bandgula". He had to be there at eight and it was already seven thirty. The slow and steady movement of the car that purred on the sleek roads had a soothing effect on him and Ashim was soon fast asleep.

TWENTY

The Wise One

If you would have visited Pataliputra Colony in Patna in 1958, you might have chanced to come upon two little girls – one four years old, chubby-cheeked, wide eyed, with two long braids falling behind, holding on tightly to the elder child's hand or frock- the other all of six years, rather tall for her age, long braids tied with ribbon, with features already moulding into sternness and dignity (after all she had a younger sister to look after) the gait exuding great confidence. The two would be a familiar sight for after school hours they would often roam around the colony which had only a score of houses then. Their positions would be so- one saying things in a confident way, the other looking up at the speaker in wonder, amazed that there could be such things. Did ever a doubt cross the mind of the little one? Never, for one could never ever doubt a person like Didi – yes, the personage is my elder sister Mira.

Our house had been newly-built and our father being the extremely foresighted person he was, provided a large garden, so we two would be pottering about in the garden or on the streets most of the time. Being with Didi was in itself a wonderful game which never ceased. Gifted with an extremely fertile imagination, a descriptive power rarely surpassed, she would dazzle the gullible me with stories she spun around herself.

"Didi, Sister Mary Laurette told us a story about a girl Cinderella, I wish I too had a fairy god-mother," I confided in her one day.

"Your wish is granted," she said solemnly.

"But how?" I asked, putting my thumb in my mouth.

"Because I am your fairy godmother," she whispered, taking my thumb out. I giggled helplessly. "Where is your wand?"

"I lost it, but," she came closer, the eyes rounded, the forehead wrinkled, the loud voice dropped to a conspiratorial whisper, "if you find it for me..." and we lost ourselves in plans.

As we grew older, I grew naughtier, Didi wiser. Any printed matter engrossed her completely and she would devour ravenously even the pages of the religious magazine "Kalyan"-- I would just admire the glossy pictures.

It was our responsibility to clean out the bedroom cupboard when we were considered big enough, when my sister was in the seventh standard and I in the fifth. We had to remove everything, dust the shelves, put in fresh newspaper and rearrange everything with a naughty brother jumping in between, and a baby sister cooing near our feet. The danger period would come when the old newspapers had to be removed. Something sometimes would catch Didi's eye, and there between the hair-oil, talcum powder, various combs and clips, and such sundry articles, the future gynaecologist would sit and just not budge until she had read all that she wanted. "Let's finish it, see Shiboo is playing with the cut-glass bowl and Manno will surely put something in her mouth," I would beg, but with a "You do it," she would again be lost and complaining angrily, I would finish it. But, this happened seldom.

It was around these times one day that my younger brother came running. "Just see what Mira Didi is doing," he panted. Ma had gone to her weekly prayer meeting and only the four of us were in the house. Fearing that she had cut or bruised herself (she was learning cycling and was famed for her bruises) I ran.

There, in the main bedroom, draped in Ma's purple Chanderi sari with anklets around her head, the pallav trailing in a glorious train, red lipstick smeared on her lips and cheeks, a faraway look in her eyes stood my sister on a stool. To us she appeared no less regal than a Mughal princess.

"What are you doing?" I gasped aghast.

"Speak politely, I am princess Mrinalini."

Poor five year old Shiboo stood dumbfounded. "Who are we then?" he wailed, worried at the identity crisis.

"You are my subjects; you will do all that is desired by me, you are my servants."

Seeing the boy's lower lip trembling, something in me stirred. May be it was then that I started administering the bitter pill which would help some hinder some.

"See if she is Princess Mrinalini then you are Prince Shivanand and I am Princess Padmavati," I placated the boy.

Undaunted, the great Mrinalini spake thus-"Ah, I have supreme powers," and what else would have issued forth I cannot say, for we could hear Ma returning. The sari was stuffed in a drawer, the anklets thrown on the top shelf and the fallen princess was hastily rubbing off lipstick.

"If you don't tell on me you get a bar of chocolate each," so not a word was said but our mother got a shock when she took the sari out to wear to a wedding next week.

Didi was brilliant even at that age. And what a multi faceted brilliance it was! She excelled in everything, essay writing, maths, map making, even embroidery. Her drawings were such that we would always be begging her to make cards. One particular incident is imprinted- it was when she had mumps. If Didi had a disease, all of us wished we could have it too, she would glorify it so much. It was such a time and she was getting bored in her room. She had to keep the door shut otherwise the latest addition to our family, our youngest brother would just crawl in. She called and I came running. "I have made a card. Let it be disinfected in the sun and then you can have it." "But what will you take for it?" The past had shown that she could be as calculating as a money-lender. "Nothing, fool," I could not believe my ears-- maybe she was really ill. Actually it was her generous nature surfacing.

Common sense, the ready wit to improvise and a certain amount of bravado, all this was used in another card incident which glorified her in my eyes. Notre Dame Academy had just started and we were the first students. We were given the best care and attention, those American nuns nearly adopted us, and every time I got a "good" in my work, Sister Mary Freda would give me a pretty card. I had quite a collection which was kept in a cardboard box in the box-room.

One day a large lizard, the garden variety, with a long tapering tail, and a poison bag near its throat, somehow managed to come in and chose my box to recline on. Who else but Didi to go for rescue?

She surveyed the situation with her hands on her waist. "The poison will enter your card in ten minutes." "Do something," I begged.

"Yes, only I can do anything to anything, but I will pick one card as charges."

"Not the one with angels and red roses?"

"Yes, the one with angels and red roses." Sadly, I gave in.

She wrinkled her brow in deep concentration and clapped. At the sudden intrusion, the lizard looked up. "Put your fingers in your ears, I have to use my magic words." The ears were not plugged well and I could swear that all she said was "Tiktiki, tiktiki, sholomono tiktiki." But the lizard was fed up and scurried off, and I had to part with my card, but how she grew in my eyes!

May be it was this incident, may be the way she helped me solve maths problems, and maybe a thousand things that in my composition work on "The person I admire most" I wrote about her. "You have to write about a great person," said Manjula Banerjee tossing her braids. "I have written about Gandhiji."

"But I haven't even seen him." I was perplexed. Sister Mary Laurette came to my rescue. "You can write about anyone dear, as long as you admire them". So I wrote about Didi. I got a "Very Good" and it was put on the bulletin board. Puffed up with all this success I went to find my sister. Pulling her to the bulletin board I showed my work. "You're stupid," she said and turned away brusquely. I still remember the shock and hurt and could not guess that beneath the brusqueness there was an unceasing source of love which she hid under her mask of gruffness. But Didi was changing and getting more difficult to understand. Once I saw her taking out a new exercise book and writing her name on it. It should not take so much time to write just "Mira Jha" so I tiptoed behind- she had written "Dr. Mira Jha, MBBS, FRCS" I couldn't resist giggling. She caught hold of the ear that was nearest to her and said, "Fools will always remain fools."

"Listen, I am setting a target for myself and I have to achieve it someday, have you ever thought what you will be."

"I won't be anything, I'll just stay at home." I blurted. So the matter was closed but Didi has got all those degrees apart from the last one, some determination!

Days flew and Didi entered Std. eight and when she spread her various books, maps, lab copies on the table it was very impressive. She did very nice needle work too. We had outgrown pottering about in the garden so the usual meeting ground would be the terrace where no younger brother or sister would clamour for attention. Didi had no patience with small children then. She was exceptionally tall for her age and so had to start wearing salwar- kameezes quite early and I felt quite sorry for her and our games would be badly hampered by them but being the introvert she was she would prefer the bathroom to cry off. I noticed that the trips to the bathroom were growing more frequent. I cornered her and we went to our favourite haunt-- beneath the mango tree, we each had our own tree and what dreams were woven sitting among the branches!

"What's wrong?" I demanded.

"They are getting me married." She said clenching her fists.

Married? The word did not register at first. This could not be happening. We were never treated like mere daughters and this seemed to be the worst sort of betrayal.

It was after her marriage that I found the silver lining in the dark cloud, my brother-in-law, a gem of a person, he is more than the in-law attached to it and so it was after all, a gain and Didi did not have to go for three years to her in law's place. She started wearing saris, had to leave Notre Dame Academy for married girls were not allowed and joined Bankipore Girl's High School and naturally shone there too. She sat for her Matric and the day she had her seventh paper my darling nephew, Gopu the apple of my eye, was born. As long as he was with us, I took charge of him and before he could start recognizing us, Didi had to leave- the three years had passed and her mother-in-law sent the customary curd and fish to signify that her daughter-in-law must be sent to her.

What a void there was after her departure! I remember not crying when she left as all my tears were already shed on the terrace and uneasily I had to don the mantle of the elder one.

Next year she took her Matric again and won the National Scholarship. I must mention that she got tremendous cooperation from her mother-in-law and her success is partly due to her.

It was in May 1969 that I was casually informed that I'd be getting married next month. As my world turned topsy-turvy, Didi came.

"You have to face it one day or the other," she said very matter of factly and it sounded more like an attack of measles or typhoid.

"But my studies," I wailed.

"Listen, stupid," she said in the way I was accustomed to, "if there is a will there is a way and if you really want to study, you will do so." Such true words and I have managed.

After her I.SC, my lovely niece, Beena was born and Didi's family was complete. She did her MBBS and then her MS and is now a famous gynaecologist. Needless to say the period in between was full of struggles, tears, triumphs but it ended in superb success. And all these years she has been a real fairy godmother to me. She'd think of ways and means to make my life happier, give me the best that she could afford at the moment and be the bulwark of strength against whom I could lean and have my batteries re-charged.

Didi is the synonym of keeping busy – working round the clock in the nursing home she set up. To her wonderful height has been added kilos that make her look the real princess Mrinalini now. Her nieces just adore her and pour all their woes in her receptive ears.

The shy, introverted, long-limbed child is now a confident, immensely successful, very matured lady who has made a name for herself in the medical arena. I have seen her in action and have been her patient too—her hands are kind and endowed with great skill. She is extremely patient—no bedside manner there—but immense patience and understanding combined with the will to eliminate all suffering. What more could a sick person desire?

If you were journeying towards Patna from the Delhi route, you would pass the station Bihta. Just near the station hangs a board proclaiming the name and degrees of my sister. If you are ill, go find her. And there, sitting behind her desk or in her O.T, a twinkle in her eye, sits the wise one- the fairy godmother to all those who visit her.

NOTES

Story-1

1. Diwali-aHindu festival of lights
2. Taj Mahal-a world famous monument, one of the seven wonders
3. laddoos-sweet
4. kaju rolls-sweet
5. salwar kameez-Indian lady`s dress
6. gulab jamuns- sweet

Story-2

1. dupatta-a long scarf worn with salwar kameez
2. chapatis-flat,unleavened bread

Story-3

1. mound-a weight of around 38kg,used in earlier times
2. Kali-Hindu goddess3
3. karahi-wok
4. rotis-chapatis
5. moksha-eternal peace
6. tarpan-water offered to ancestors by males on the annual days of mourning

7. shraddh-annual days of mourning when ancestors are offered water and worshipped
8. tulsi-basil

Story-4

1. none

Story-5

1. sindoor-vermillion-if put in a woman`s parting of hair is symbolic of marriage
2. bhabhi-brothers wife
3. juhi-fragrant,white flower
4. dhoti-kurta-male dress worn by Hindu men not common among the young
5. sindoordan-the ritual of putting vermillion in the parting of hair of the bride by the groom, signifying marriage

Story-6

1. makki roti- corn chapatti (bread)
2. daru-cheap liquor
3. ghaghra-choli-long skirt and blouse
4. jai jai-a greeting

Story-7

1. phiran-long,loose woollen top worn by Kashmiri women
2. mirch-chili
3. Bihari Babu-man from the state of Bihar, spoken teasingly

4. Shatrughan Sinha- actor from Bihar
5. litti chokha- a food of Bihar
6. roganjosh-food of Kashmir
7. kebab-meat rolls
8. ghee-clarified butter
9. arahar dal- cooked pigeon pea
10. alu gobhi subzi-potato, cauliflower curry
11. babua-endearment meaning little son
12. fauji-army man
13. parathas-triangular chapatis fried in ghee
14. yakhni-Kashmiri food

Story-8

1. Vrindavan ,Varanasi-ancient ,holy cities where widows were sent earlier
2. sadhu-holy man
3. dadra,thumri-Indian classical style of singing
4. Apka diya khatein hain-literally-we eat what you provide-a very polite way of giving thanks to someone very superior
5. chik-blinds
6. Rajmata-queen mother
7. choolah-mud oven fuelled by coal
8. pallu-the end of the sari which falls from the shoulder

Story-9

1. burqa-a black outer garment worn by Muslim ladies which only shows the eyes
2. ek minute-just a minute

3. rakhi-a festival when the sister ties a golden string on her brother`s wrist and is promised protection all her life
4. Sardarni-lady of the sikh religion
5. Behenji-sister
6. bhajan-hymn
7. Madhuri Dixit-A very beautiful actress
8. Vishvmitra-Menaka-a holy sage whose penance was broken by the beauty of Menaka who was sent to do so

Story-10

1. none

Story-11

1.none

Story-12

1. Kumbh snan-a very holy period which comes after every twelve years when a bath in the Ganga is washing all sins
2. mujra- a dance by a courtesan
3. Lucknavi-from Lucknow, a famous city
4. Kathak-a classical Indian dance
5. ghunghroo-bells worn on the ankles when dancing
6. khala-aunt {urdu}
7. mela-fair
8. sherbet-a sweet drink
9. jee- saying yes politely
10. bapuji-father

11. Navratan set- necklace and earrings studded with the nine gems
12. didi-elder sister
13. Lakshmi-goddess of wealth
14. amma-mother
15. dadaji-grandfather
16. bhagwan ka lakh lakh shukr hai-a thousand thanks to the almighty

Story-13

1. kheer-a sweet dish made out of rice and milk
2. baba-father or sometimes grandfather

Story-14

1. Bengali-from the state of Bengal
2. Maithil-from the land of Mithila
3. Brahmin-the highest caste
4. Mithilanchal-the area of Mithila
5. baratis-people in a marriage procession
6. barat-marriage procession
7. Durga-goddess of war
8. champa- a fragrant flower, pale cream
9. Tagore songs-songs written by the great Bengali poet
10. Hemant Kumar -a very famous singer

Story-15

1. dadas-mafia
2. chachi-aunt
3. shlokas-couplets in Sanskrit

4. 15th August-India's Independence day
5. Lal Qila-the Red Fort-a very famous monument
6. garibi-poverty

Story-16

1. chalna hai didi-will you come, sister
2. ladki hai-Its a girl
3. kaun hai,arey koi hai-who is there, is there somebody?
4. chadar-sheet
5. lota- a container for water
6. salwar- clothes to cover the legs
7. arrey,chai lao- bring tea

Story-17

1. RJD- a political party
2. khao,piyo mast raho-eat, drink and be merry
3. FM-Finance Minister
4. HM-Home Minister
5. Hum se hai zamana,zamane se hum nahin- famous Urdu couplet showing the empowerment of a group

Story-18

1. none

Story-19

1. Shiamak Davar- a modern Indian dance director
2. bundgala- a formal coat